THE RISING

BOOK FOUR IN THE CALLING SERIES

L.C. PYE

The Rising

Copyright © 2025 by L.C. Pye

Contact Info: authorl.c.pye@gmail.com

Front Cover Design by: Selkkie Designs

Editor: E&A Editing Services

ISBN: 979-8-9879746-7-4

THE RISING

BOOK FOUR IN THE CALLING SERIES

L.C. PYE

LiftedLines Press

SIGN UP FOR MY

AUTHOR NEWSLETTER

Be the first to learn about L.C. Pye's new releases and receive exclusive content.

Dedicated to those who are rising from the ashes. Beauty can be found there.

KINGDOM
NORTH
KINGDOM OF TRO'ISH
KARDEN
BANESMYTH
HATTLEE
THE CLEARING
GASMERE

F LANDORE
AYDENCIA
MOUNTAINS
LLYCIA
KINGDOM OF
NEFALI
CYPERIAN
SEA
KINGDOM OF
VASDERE

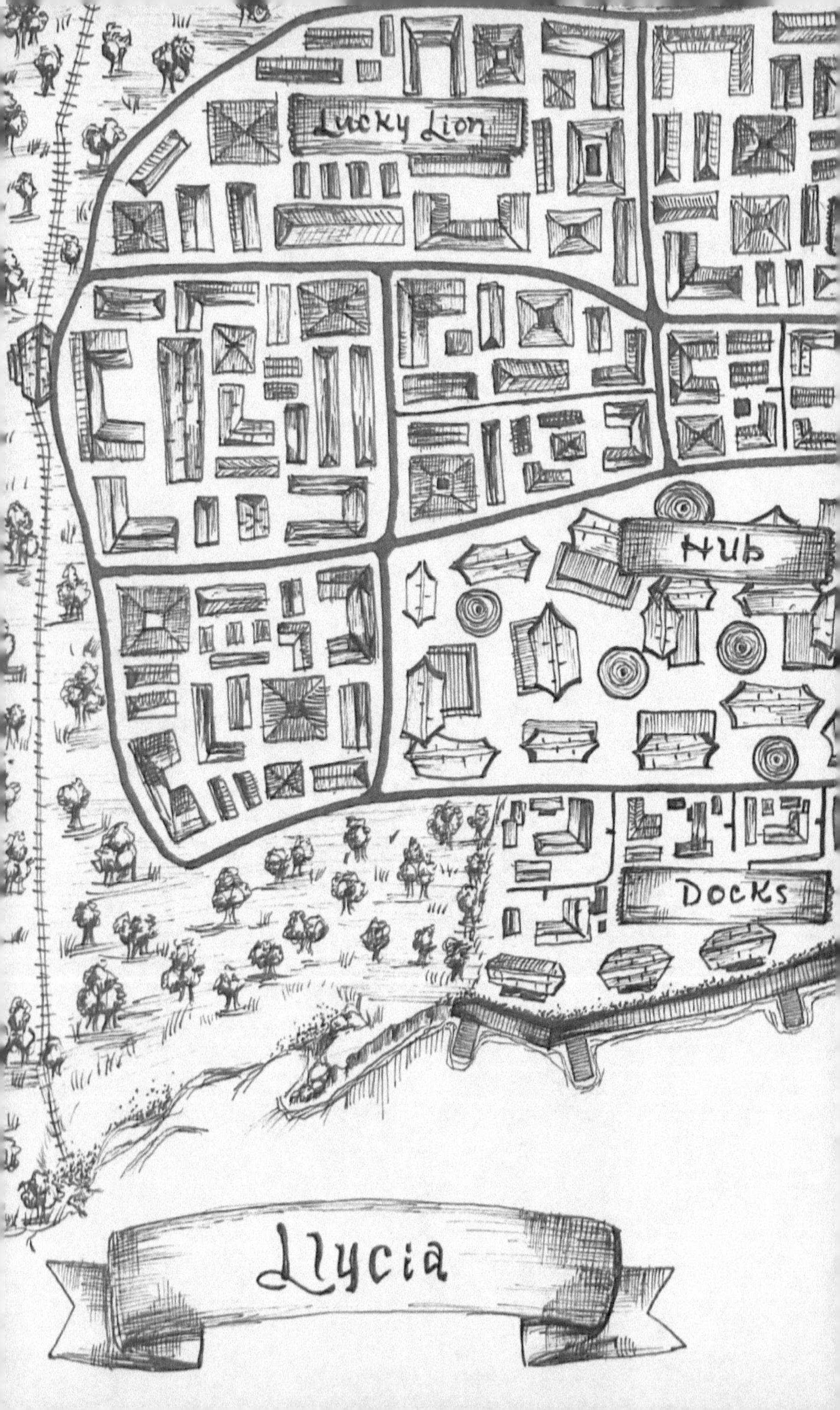

Lucky Lion
Hub
Docks
Llycia

N
W
S
Mead
King's Court

CHAPTER 1

Talia

WATER DRIPPED DOWN THE stone walls and splattered into growing puddles, drowning out our procession deeper into the mountain of Skyhall. The storm hadn't let up in days and neither had the circular talks in the so-called war room.

The older guard, leading me down the tunnel, stepped aside and stationed himself beside the roughly carved doorway, waiting for me to enter. I slowed my steps and took a deep breath. The guard bowed as I passed. Muffled voices of Aydencian leaders filled the room as they sat at a round table, deep in conversation.

Alon noticed me first. "Your Highness," he said with a smile that had once felt comforting. Like an echo, his greeting was repeated by the other five leaders, the same leaders who were always present for these meetings.

Inhaling, I relaxed my jaw and tipped my head similarly to how Prince Kasper would. "Have you heard anything?" I asked as I walked to an empty chair, opposite of Alon.

Alon's smile fell, but only for a moment, before anyone could notice. "No, Your Highness. The weather continues to hinder our communications with the mainland. As has been the case for the last four days."

I clenched the back of the chair and nodded. I had asked the same question every day since my return from our failed rescue mission, and Alon always gave me the same answer. However, this back and forth would have to end. One day the answers would change.

"Ah, Captain Dareon, good." Richard stood. "Welcome."

Alon was the first to break our stalemate, his gaze shifting past my shoulder to the captain. It took those in the room a moment of watching Captain Dareon sit before they noticed I still stood behind my chair. Once they did, I finally slid into it, swallowing the disgust from using that move to gain some sort of control. It reminded me of King Madden.

"We have been talking in circles these last few days," Richard continued with a strained laugh as though we had spent the time arguing over what dessert to serve. Some of the other leaders chuckled too, attempting to lighten the mood of the room. Hidden under the table, I squeezed my hands until they ached. "But all of us know what is at stake here, and it's imperative we consider every option before enacting a plan."

"Captain Dareon, I asked for your presence today," Alon drew everyone's eyes as he spoke directly to the captain, "to share with us a rough estimate of how many warriors are ready to be deported at this moment."

I blinked, unsure if I had heard correctly as everyone else twisted back toward Richard. "It might aid us in our decision on the best towns to send them to once this storm passes and we can move forward."

"Of course, sir." Captain Dareon's gruff voice sliced through the room, pulling my attention back onto his broad, weather-worn face.

"I thought we weren't going to infiltrate the villages until we rescued my father, Jules, and Gil?" I cut in, resisting the urge to squirm under the scrutiny of the leaders who disliked my interruptions on a good day. "We agreed they are our first priority." I leveled Alon with a stare. "What happened to not wanting any unnecessary bloodshed?"

"Of course, Your Highness." Alon gave a tight smile. "This is a preventative measure, as we have previously mentioned. Our warriors will need to be there when the time comes to protect the villagers." The orange glow from the torches cast a shadow over Alon's face, making his eyes appear darker and hardened.

Ignoring the desire to make myself smaller, I leaned forward. "And as I mentioned before, there will be far less bloodshed if we kill the only man necessary to end this."

A muffled cough pulled my attention toward the doorway where two warriors stood on guard. I wasn't sure when they had arrived, but I narrowed my eyes at the familiar face of the one who had coughed. Raph stared back at me. He hadn't spoken to me since we got back four days ago. What annoyed me even more was that I knew what he was silently trying to communicate to me, *Don't push them.*

"Your Highness, please consider." Of course Richard jumped in, again. "If we go that route, there will potentially be more innocent lives in the line of fire. My son, your friend, and your father."

I opened my mouth to object again but stopped. They had already made their decision.

"We also want them rescued as soon as possible," Hanna added with her gentle voice. The blood boiling in my veins rushed to my cheeks. She'd hardly spoken since we returned with the news that Gil was one of those captured by Prince Kasper. Dark circles lived permanently underneath her eyes. "However, we must be strategic about this—even if it hurts us." Her gaze never lifted from the map, as though it would reveal the answers we needed.

Taking the silence as his cue, Captain Dareon directed his report to Alon, disclosing the number of warriors ready and how many could pass as ready if perhaps stationed with superior officers. He then drew everyone's attention to the map covering most of the table. Everybody leaned in and began pointing and prodding at the different figurines, arguing about which villages were best to station the warriors in. For a moment it was almost easy to see it all as simply a game.

"Wait," I muttered. "This won't work!" My raised voice broke through their noise.

"Your Highness?" Richard didn't look up. He just moved another wooden piece across the map.

"If this was about protecting the villagers of Landore, you wouldn't be arguing over which villages are worthy of protection, because they all are. What is this really about?"

They finally looked in my direction, staring at me as if I was speaking another language. But their silence was confirmation enough. Still, I wanted them to admit they were keeping me in the dark.

"What aren't you telling me?" I reiterated.

Alon finally responded, "Every village will have protection." He straightened. "This is simply the first round. There will be more. Depending on you."

"How so?" I studied him wearily.

He sat back down. The others followed suit. "As soon as the weather clears, we need you to join Nadav and Hafsa and leave for Nefali to finalize our alliance with the king and queen."

My heart jumped into my throat. "No," I choked, "not before we rescue the others. That was the plan. Couldn't Hafsa and Nadav go alone?" I quickly added. "Surely they would find more success with their king and queen than me. Or any one of you." I extended my hand out toward every one of them around the table. "You all know the rebellion better."

"If that were the case, we would not be at our current standstill," Richard said. "They want to meet the Lost Princess of Landore."

"Meeting me will most likely result in the alliance failing." I waved a hand at myself, emphasizing how unprincess-like I was.

"That can be amended," Richard countered, then he nodded at Hanna. "Dear, didn't you mention a few gowns were being preserved for such an occasion."

"Yes. And I can gather some jewels from the other noble families," Hanna answered.

A snort came from the elderly man in charge of Aydencia's treasury. My interruptions weren't the only common occurrence at these meetings. The man often found something to scoff at, thinking he knew best since he had previously been on the late royal council.

Richard glared at the elderly man, who reluctantly dipped his head toward Hanna. "Problem solved," Richard said with a beaming smile. "Plus, you've already been trained in how to act like a princess."

Heat radiated off my skin. He had no idea what I endured at King Madden's hand.

"The weather should clear any day, Your Highness. So be prepared." Richard folded his hands as if that sealed the deal.

"No," I gasped, shaking my head. "No. You told me I just needed to be *here* to give hope, and I agreed because," I turned my attention to Alon, "you promised to save my loved ones. I didn't come here to trade one gilded cage for another."

Richard coughed as if he had choked on some spit.

"We are working on saving them, Your Highness," Alon said calmly, but his face remained tight.

"Not quick enough."

"As much as we wish," Alon glanced toward Hanna and Richard, "we cannot simply snap our fingers and rescue loved ones."

"You did with me," I said.

"And it revealed our hand. Now we have fewer resources at the palace."

"There must—"

"What exactly do you think we should do, Your Highness?" Alon asked, raising one brow at me.

"We...we..." My gaze darted across the map, wishing it might give me some grand idea. "We could trick Madden by letting him believe he is in control again."

"Continue..." Alon's face didn't give anything away.

I lowered my voice, trying to sound confident. "We will promise to disperse the Northern Rebels."

A loud laugh broke out.

"You can't be serious?" Richard asked with raised eyebrows. "Princess Talia," he bowed his head, "he will never take your word on that. He will want evidence the Northern Rebels are no more. He will want blood."

"Not if he believes the rebels are calling for a ceasefire and will support him as king," I countered.

"And how would you achieve that?" Richard asked.

I glanced at the map again, heart hammering. The thought was certifiably insane. But it was my choice. "By becoming queen. By marrying Prince Kasper," I blurted.

Objections broke out in the room, but the sound of Raph clearing his throat rang the loudest.

"Absolutely not." Richard threw up his arms.

Alon raised his hand and met my gaze. "That would convince Madden he is back in control because he would be." His stare pinned me in place. "It would be foolish to allow him to have you in his control again, *Your Highness.*"

I didn't miss the way he said my title like a parent reprimanding a child. "But I could help," I said, not willing to cave. "I could discover where Gil, my father, and Jules are being kept."

Alon exhaled and Richard pinched the bridge of his nose. "Again, we already have spies stationed in the palace doing exactly that. Though not as many as we'd like," Richard said.

"But—"

Alon cut me off. "Can everyone please excuse us?"

They fell quiet and exchanged a few glances. I stared at the map, wishing the blush heating my cheeks didn't blatantly share my embarrassment as their chairs scraped against the stone floor.

The footsteps stopped and I was about to look back up when Alon added, "You too, Raph."

"Sir."

"It is an order."

It was worse waiting for Raph's footsteps to disappear.

Alon stood and circled the table. "Your mother is a Healer, right?"

I frowned. "Yes?"

"I assume you have witnessed her work on occasion?" he asked, knowing the answer himself. He couldn't have forgotten what I had done in Hattlee.

"A few times," I said, not divulging the fact I had spent most of my childhood watching and assisting her.

"Then perhaps you might understand that a bone protruding out of a person's ankle might seem dire and the obvious place you should focus your attention on first, but a good Healer knows to take in the rest of the body too and search for signs of anything more critical, like a head wound. Then they might have other Healers assist in bandaging the smaller wounds so they can focus on the more life threatening one." Alon sat in the open chair next to me.

"I'm not a Healer," I shrugged.

"No, but you understand what I'm getting at, right?" He tilted his head as though to hear my response, but didn't wait for it. "Rescuing Gil, Jules, and your father are sort of like that bone. It needs to be remedied. However, we already have skilled men and women focusing on that. You getting involved would hinder their success. But you can be invaluable to them, and to us all, by going to Nefali and getting their support to help ensure we overthrow Madden with as little bloodshed as possible. This is your calling."

I stared at the map again until my eyes went blurry. I didn't want to put more distance between myself and them. But I needed to do something. Anything to help that was more than sitting in on these meetings and being a face for them to be paraded around.

"Okay," I relented.

Alon dipped his head toward me. "I knew you would understand." A pleased smile took over his face. "I would suggest you inform your mother. If the weather clears, you could be leaving as early as tomorrow," he said, standing.

I watched him walk out of the room before dropping my head into my hands. I was exhausted. All of it was exhausting. Taking a slow breath in, I lifted my head and placed my hands on the armrests, ready to stand. I peered at the map with every village of Landore on it and knew I was in way over my head. I didn't know how to strategize or win a war. Apparently, all I knew was how to be impulsive and endanger those I loved. I closed my eyes, hoping to push down the wave of guilt. Turning from the table, I walked out of the small, dark room.

My pace increased once outside, trying to alleviate the time spent this deep in the mountain.

"...We can't keep ignoring it." I froze at a bend in the hallway. The voice sounded frustrated and almost desperate. I peeked around the corner, enough to see the leader of Aydencia's civic affairs grasping Richard's arm.

"If we don't address it, we may lose the narrative, or worse...control over the matter."

Richard huffed. "I won't say this again. We will not legitimize the rumors by bringing attention to it." He pulled his arm free and stormed down the hallway. The other man stood frozen, staring at his empty hand before heading in the same direction Richard had gone.

I released my breath and along with it the tension from that exchange. With a slower pace, I made my way to the main hallway at the front of the mountain.

The fresh sound of boots hitting the stone floor had me glancing back to discover Raph closing the distance between us.

"Leave me alone," I said over my shoulder.

His steps didn't cease. "I want to talk."

I turned and stopped. "Now you want to talk?" Raph halted inches from me. Heat traveled up my neck, remembering what happened the last time we were this close. I stepped back. "What about the past four days? You've had plenty of chances to talk." I turned away only to spin back around. "And I don't need you giving me not-so-subtle hints that you don't agree with me. I don't want your opinion. Especially, when you don't even seem to care about Gil, Jules, and my father getting rescued."

His expression remained frozen as I waited for him to tell me I was wrong.

"You know what, it doesn't matter." I walked away, but his footsteps quickened behind me.

His hand wrapped around my arm, pulling me to slow down.

I yanked it from his grip. "Raph, just leave me alone." My voice cracked. I took off down the women's wing. I didn't want him to see how much he affected me. How hurt I was by him shutting me out.

I opened my door and slammed it shut before he could catch up. My breathing was erratic as I walked to my bed only to spot a large box placed on it. Another dress for another dinner party I would need to make an *appearance* at. With a frustrated groan I grabbed the box ready to throw it across the room.

Knock. Knock.

I jumped and dropped the box back on the bed. Frustration burned into anger as I stormed toward the door. Wind brushed against my face when I threw it open, ready to command Raph to leave me alone.

"Oh. Mother," I said, blinking rapidly. "I thought you were someone else."

"I heard voices," she said carefully. "Things sounded...heated?"

I stiffened, heat climbing up my neck.

"Is everything all right? Are you okay?"

My strength gave way like a candle burned to nothing. "Not really," I murmured, stepping aside to let her in.

She crossed to the bed and sat down, patting the space beside her. When I joined her, she took my hand. Her touch was light but steady, tethering me.

"They won't listen to anything I say," I exhaled. "They seem to care less and less about saving Father, Jules, and Gil. And now they want me to go to Nefali to be some spokesperson for their war."

Her hand tightened around mine. "Talia, I'm so sorry."

I looked at her, but her eyes stayed fixed on our joined hands.

"For what? None of this is your fault. You're not the one sending me away. You're not the reason they're still in Madden's hands."

She released her hand from mine. "No. But I feel as though it's my fault all this has happened to you."

My chest tightened. "What do you mean?"

For a moment she didn't speak, and when she did, her voice sounded far away. "That night in the forest...the night we found you."

"Yes, what about it?"

"We said you were abandoned, and a group of Hunters found you..."

"Right, then you and Father offered to adopt me. I know." We didn't talk about that night often, but growing up, Jacob Martin never let me forget it. How my own parents hadn't wanted me.

"Well. The thing is…" She licked her lips and swallowed. "That's not exactly what happened."

I lowered my chin. "What *exactly* happened then?"

"I found you in the forest."

"Okay…why would you lie about that?"

"Because you weren't alone."

My heart slammed against my ribs.

"There was a woman with you," she went on. "She was hurt badly. She wouldn't let me help her, no matter how I tried." Mother had a far off look in her eyes and then she looked at me. "At first she tried to hide you from me, clutching you so tightly I almost didn't see you were there at all. But then," her gaze drifted, remembering, "something spooked her and she begged me to take you. She demanded it, and made me promise to keep you safe." She swallowed hard. "And I promised. I didn't ask questions or anything. I just took you, believing it was a miracle. That John and I would finally have a child of our own." Her eyes grew misty. "I thought our love would be enough. But as you grew and the villagers saw how different you looked, I realized I'd already failed her promise in keeping you safe. I watched them mock you, isolate you, and every time you came home with another bruise, I felt her words echoing in my head. *Keep her safe.* I had broken that woman's demand. I was never able to keep you safe."

"I…I…" My mouth was dry. "I don't know what to say."

She grabbed my hand again, her fingers trembling but strong. "I know how hard your life has been. And I wish more than anything I could have protected you from all of that pain. But through it you have become the strong, brave woman who sits in front of me."

"I don't feel—"

Her grip tightened, forcing me to look at her. "You can handle anything they throw at you. Not because of who they think you should be, but because of who you already are. Stay true to yourself."

CHAPTER 2

Jules

My boots caught on the uneven ground, and I pitched forward, hissing when the rope cut deeper into my raw wrists. The guard who had my rope secured around his saddle peered over his shoulder with an annoyed look. I flashed him my teeth as though the rope burn along my wrists or even the dirt I felt caked to my face didn't bother me at all. It did though. And it was getting harder every day to hide how it was affecting me.

I nearly broke when Gil glanced back, brow furrowed, mouth pouted in concern.

The guilt smacking me hurt more than the open wounds on my wrists. I'm sure I looked like a mess after days of traveling by foot, a trail of blood in my wake, but he was in far worse shape. The red slash bisecting his bottom lip was too vibrant against his pale lips. But that was easier to look at than his swollen eye, a mottled purple like a rotting plum. A display of last night's "questioning" with the King's Wraith. The first few nights Gil would return with no physical evidence of being tortured. The King's Wraith seemed to be growing more desperate with each mile that we got closer to the palace. I slammed my teeth together, watching Gil trip over his feet as he turned back around.

"Halt!"

The tiny bit of slack in the rope was instant relief. Taking the moment where I didn't need to concentrate on keeping up with the vigorous pace we were forced to endure, I stepped to the side until I could spot Talia's father toward the front. His injured foot forced the King's Wraith to give him a horse to avoid him slowing us down. However, the horse was tethered to another guard's, preventing any chance of escape. Talia's father twisted in his saddle, searching through the guards until he spotted me and Gil. Meeting my eye, he gave a thin-lipped smile, as though hoping to encourage us to keep going. I was glad John seemed to be treated better. Nonetheless, I moved back out of his line of sight, too tired and sore to hold onto my own wan smile.

I eyed the guard who held the other end of my rope, anticipating being dragged to a nearby tree to be tied up for the night, but no one dismounted. The sun beating down on my back told me it was too early to be stopping for the night. I looked at Gil, he was already watching me.

At my arched brow, silently asking why the sudden change from rushing to get back to Llycia, he lifted his chin and looked at the tops of the trees.

The blue sky had a gray tint to it, but it didn't resemble the signs of a storm coming. My stomach tightened, not wanting to accept what my instincts were telling me.

"Dismount!" The King's Wraith ordered. He sounded closer than usual.

A black horse trotted up and stopped between Gil and me.

"Tie them up for now. And be ready to move out quickly." With a tight rein, the King's Wraith directed his horse to turn around and galloped toward the front, kicking up dust that blew back at us.

I narrowed my eyes, keeping him in my line of sight as he made his way to the front. The rope around my wrists pulled tight again, and I gasped in pain as I pitched forward onto my knees. Struggling to my feet, I tried to slacken the tension and followed the guard to a tree. A strong yank had me on the forest floor again, but this time I remained. While the guard was busy securing the rope around the tree, I stole the opportunity to scoot a few inches farther to get more slack, hoping he wouldn't notice.

Gil watched me with a smirk that disappeared with a wince as his guard tied him to his tree. Like usual, they positioned him about ten feet away from me, and John even further away. I dropped my head to my chest and stared at the individual blades of grass underneath me, then I began my ritual for the past five days of counting them. I only let my mind focus on one blade at a time to drown out the commotion around me.

"Who's riding in?" The guard in charge of watching me broke through my concentration.

"I think they said another unit," Gil's guard answered back.

The number I had been on vanished as I peered up and caught Gil eyeing the two guards. We hadn't come across anyone yet, so I had assumed they were staying as far away from the villages as possible.

Horse hooves echoed throughout the trees. We had stopped in a small clearing, and I could see the uncertainty on the guards' faces as they eyed the tree line. The King's Wraith and Sal faced the direction the commotion seemed to be coming from. Finally, two horses broke through the trees with King's Guards on their backs, followed by five others. They stopped in front of the King's Wraith and dismounted. Each dropped to a knee.

"Your Highness," the first guard spoke with a deep voice. He isolated himself from the others by standing.

"Lieutenant Revel," the King's Wraith said with a tip of his head, and Sal, who stood next to him, shifted his weight at the guard's name. "What brings you and my father's men here?"

The lieutenant stepped forward, his chest lifted. He looked out among the other guards in our company as if he was taking stock of cattle before his gaze landed on John, Gil, and me.

The bark from the tree scratched my back as I pressed against it.

Lieutenant Revel was a model of what one might imagine a person in charge would look like. His tall, athletic stature and dominating presence made Sal and even the King's Wraith pale in comparison.

"The king has ordered me to demonstrate to the villagers what will happen if they offer help to the rebels." His booming voice was loud enough for everyone to hear. "He believes they've forgotten what happens when loyalty falters." Lieutenant Revel ended with his eyes locked on Sal and the King's Wraith.

Sal placed his hand on the pommel of his sword, but the King's Wraith stayed motionless. His back didn't even move in response to his breath. Everyone, besides those in Lieutenant Revel's company, seemed frozen.

"I'm sure you are fulfilling my father's orders with the utmost efficiency," the King's Wraith said, breaking the tension.

"Of course." The lieutenant dipped his head. "I would be honored if you and your company," the lieutenant's eyes found the three of us again, "joined us in the village we are occupying. I assume you are making your way back to Llycia." He waited for the King's Wraith to confirm his assumption, yet he remained silent.

"I'm sure King Madden would expect an update on our progress, plus it isn't half a day's ride from here," the lieutenant added.

Everyone seemed to hold their breath as we waited for the King's Wraith to say or do something.

Finally he spoke. "We will spend the evening in the village, but we will be gone by first light. There are urgent matters that require our presence in Llycia right away."

"Of course, Your Highness. We are honored," the lieutenant said, placing his fist over his chest for a shallow bow. He and the men who came with him remounted their horses.

The King's Wraith nodded at Sal who barked orders for everyone to mount up. My guard untied my ropes as the lieutenant and his men disappeared. I remained focused on the treeline trying to understand how this Lieutenant Revel could have the power to influence the King's Wraith and throw him off course.

We traveled through the forest and it wasn't long before my instincts were screaming at me because a storm wasn't coming. The sky was gray because of smoke. I thought a camp of the King's Guard would be the worst thing to enter into, but it was nothing compared to the memories of Gasmere that were flooding my mind. I couldn't help but think we were about to walk through the front gates of my village, and I would witness the devastation and destruction all over again.

I coughed into my sleeve, and tried to wipe the water from my eyes to see better. We were coming up to the village's gate. Scorch marks coated what was left of the beam marking the entrance, and I was unable to make out the name of the village. I wanted to gag as the horses kicked up the ashes, coating me in them.

Gil and I were last to enter the village, but everyone else remained on their horses in the middle of the village's penta, or what was left of it. My heels dug into the ground, and a hot pain ran up my arm as I pulled against my restraints, trying to take in the tragedy around me.

Everything was gone.

In Gasmere, the King's Wraith and his men had left the penta mostly untouched, focusing their destruction mainly in the individual quarters. But here...

The ruins of the stalls with some of the metal items were in a pile of ash on the ground. A flicker of movement to my left caught my eye. I thought it might have been a villager, but it was gone before I could tell. Burnt beams leaned against one another haphazardly, taking up a large area of the penta. It must have been the village's Meeting House where the Elders met.

"Welcome to Hattlee," Lieutenant Revel announced from atop his horse.

I blinked rapidly and my breath grew shallow. This...this couldn't be.

I sought out Gil a few feet away from me, his face was near the same color as the ash swirling around.

"This village is the second one we have occupied, and I can assure you they were in dire need of a lesson, Your Highness." The lieutenant tightened his grip on the reins. "When we arrived, you couldn't tell one calling from the other, they were all mixed."

The lieutenant looked at the King's Wraith with an arched eyebrow, waiting for *something*. There was something in the Wraith's stillness that didn't feel like indifference. And that unsettled me more.

"Can you even imagine how a village got to this point?" Lieutenant Revel asked.

"I cannot," the King's Wraith said flatly. "My father will be more than pleased to hear of what you have accomplished."

Lieutenant Revel tipped his head forward.

"What of the quarters? Is there anything left?" the King's Wraith asked, looking in the direction of the Healer's quarter. You could still see the faint symbol for the Healer's etched into the burnt archway.

"We kept the village's tavern untouched," the lieutenant relayed. "We would have only flogged enough folks to get the message to sink in, but we discovered the village had been housing rebel sympathizers from Gasmere."

I caved inward as my chest squeezed. Air couldn't reach my lungs as I tried to gulp in more of it.

"Breathe." Gil's voice, but it was distant, and it didn't do anything to help my current state.

"I...I—" I choked on the words. "I was supposed to protect them—" Pain shot through my knees as I crashed against the hard ground, but it was quickly replaced with the panic I felt.

"Something seems wrong with one of your prisoners." The lieutenant's voice reached my ears, but it sounded distorted.

Someone said something else, but I couldn't comprehend it.

My mind screamed at me to breathe or I would die.

But my body wouldn't listen. I fought for my breath.

Freezing water rushed over my head.

I took a sharp inhale.

My hair covered my face as water dripped from it, but at least I could breathe. I placed my bound hands on the ground, letting them sink into the muddy water. Hidden behind my hair, I took two slow breaths before I had the courage to look up.

Gil was in front of me with a pinched face, and a guard stood off to the side with a bucket in his hands. Everyone else had disappeared.

"Are you okay?" Gil asked.

I averted my gaze, guilt biting deeper than the cold.

CHAPTER 3

Kasper

LAUGHTER ECHOED OFF THE walls and mingled with the thud of mugs slamming against wood. The air buzzed with heat and ale-slicked breath as my men unfastened their inhibitions like belts and gave in to drink. I would have rather suffered through one of my father's trainings than be there, but that wasn't an option. Revel had my father's ear and would no doubt be sending a report to him about our interaction. I had to put on a show.

"The villagers?" At my question, Lieutenant Revel, who sat across the table from me, raised a confused brow. I added, "Are there many left?"

"Enough. Enough at least to rebuild and be fine." He gave a noncommittal shrug. "They've been keeping to their quarters."

I nodded slowly, jaw tight.

A young lady who seemed too young for the job, approached our table, laden with more than our ales. The other men around me leered and made comments, each one causing her strained smile to flicker. None of them seemed to have noticed the red around her eyes. I dropped my chin as she set down four ales. Grabbing one, I kept my gaze lowered until she was gone.

"Long live the king!" Lieutenant Revel lifted his drink in the middle of the table.

"Long live the king." The words left my mouth automatically, joining the others.

Sal's voice boomed above the rest. He stood and slammed his mug to the table, face red from drink.

"And the body count?" I asked, setting my drink down casually.

"Some have fled, but Sergeant W," Revel nodded at the guard to my left, "visited the Healer's quarter this morning."

The mug's rough wood dug into my palm as my grip tightened.

"Your Highness." Sergeant W bowed his head. "Due to the lack of Healers in the village and their Healing House being destroyed, they have had difficulties caring for their wounded."

Hiding my hands under the table, I dug my fingernails into the tops of my thighs. "The count?"

"There have been thirty-five reported wounded and twelve in critical condition," Sergeant W answered.

"And the refugees you mentioned?" I moved my attention to the nearest group of guards.

"The youths are in quarantine, and the adults were given a vivid display of what would happen if they didn't swear their loyalty to the king," Revel answered with a smug grin.

I grunted, hiding my face with my mug as I downed the bitter ale. Out of the corner of my eye, Sal tensed as he downed whatever was left in his mug and signaled for the barkeep to bring another.

"And how is your mission progressing so far, Your Highness?" Revel asked, a smirk poorly hidden by the top of his mug. "Any closer to rescuing our princess?"

Revel and Sal stared at me with dark, haughty eyes. They were nothing more than vultures, circling, waiting for me to mess up. Having played this game for too long, I savored my sip and leaned back in my seat. They tilted forward. "I have a few leads that will bring about the princess's safe return."

"Wonderful," Revel said, but his eyes remained narrowed. "I'm assuming these leads have to do with the prisoners slowing you down?"

"They're worth the slower pace," I answered flatly.

"Where did you pick them up?" Revel asked.

Drawing moisture into my mouth, I swallowed. "We heard word a group of rebels had captured Princess Talia's birth parents. We tracked them to Banesmyth and captured two of them while rescuing the princess's fath—"

Sal cut in, "It wasn't until my men and I arrived that His Highness was able to secure them." His eyes flicked toward Lieutenant Revel, who didn't peer up from his drink. Sal's hand shook as he formed a fist.

The corner of my lips lifted ever so slightly. In the past two years, my father had depended on him more and more, and it had made Sal paranoid and jealous.

The silence lingered.

"I assume then, Your Highness," Revel lifted his gaze, "you're hoping to extract some information from those rebels since you are keeping them alive?"

Revel was one of my father's men I tried to steer clear of because he was intrusive and too perceptive.

"Yes," I answered.

"How are the nightly interrogations going, Your Highness?" Sal asked with a sweetness to his words that turned bitter instantly.

Revel's eyebrows rose as he waited for my response.

"I'd assumed the notorious King's Wraith would have gotten all he needed by now," Sal baited.

Sal's words hung heavy, but I wasn't going to bite. I had grown up with his insecure threats.

Revel chuckled, low and sharp. "Careful, Sal. Challenging the heir can sound a lot like doubting the king's judgment."

Sal's face flushed darker, his fist tightening on the table. "My loyalty is unquestionable."

"Unquestionable men don't usually need to say it aloud," Revel drawled.

Sergeant W, who had fixated on his drink for most of the conversation, let out an abrupt laugh and then covered it with a cough.

Sal leaned forward, his voice sharp enough to cut. "Who did the king trust to help uncover the identity of the lost princess?" His fist curled against the table. "And when Vasderian spies crossed our border, who drove them out before they could poison our ranks? Me. My men."

Revel arched a brow, the corner of his mouth curving. "And who, during the year of the rain shortage, managed to secure twice the grain from the villages, saving the kingdom from starvation? I believe you and your men weren't even able to come up with a bushel." Revel leaned back in his chair. "Besides the king rewards results, Sal, not boasts of past glories."

Their voices clashed like steel. Brag after brag, strike after strike. My temples throbbed. Every word was a reminder of the game I'd been forced to grow up in. A game of power and control.

I pushed back ready to excuse myself when the door creaked open. Three men from the village slipped inside, heads bowed, the lines of exhaustion etched deep into their faces. They kept to the wall, edging toward the barkeep.

A guard at an outer table stuck out his boot, tripping one of the men. The other guards around roared with laughter as the villager pushed to his feet. "Watch your step, rat," the guard spat.

The villager muttered an apology and scurried away with his friends, but not before another guard kicked out the chair beside him, blocking the path. "Not your place, villager."

More laughter. Mugs slammed. The villagers endured it, keeping their heads down as they moved around the chair.

But not everyone was laughing. At a nearby table, a pair of young guards sat stiff in their seats, their eyes fixed on the jeering. One clenched his jaw hard enough the muscle ticked in his cheek. The other gripped his mug until his knuckles whitened. They said nothing, but the tension rolled off them. Not so long ago, they had been those villagers.

Sal's voice boomed again, desperate to drown out Revel. "And whose name is still spoken with fear in the palace halls? Whose men are the most trusted at the palace gates?"

Revel didn't blink. "For now."

I finished the last of my drink, trying to wash down the taste of rot from their power match, and stood.

"Leaving us already, Your Highness?" Sal asked, eyes glittering.

I set my mug down, letting the sound cut through the noise. "Enjoy your victories." I turned and walked out.

The night air struck cool against my skin, cleansing, though it couldn't wash away the heaviness pressing down on me. Behind me, the laughter carried on, swelling louder. I let the noise fade as I crossed the street, boots crunching over gravel and dirt. The tavern's glow dimmed behind me, swallowed by shadow, until the barn rose ahead. The scent of hay and horse drifted on the breeze, familiar and steady.

Here, at least, there was no contest, no circling vultures hungry for power. Just the quiet shuffle of hooves and the soft nickers that greeted me like an old friend. I let out a heavy breath.

"Not a pleasant evening then?"

I jolted upright, searching for the low, raspy voice that spoke out.

Talia's father sat leaning against the stable wall with a pile of hay elevating his foot. He stared at me with a strange look, one I had only ever seen Mistress Pennier give me. "More pleasant than yours."

"Ah, but I am enjoying myself. I've been a farmer my whole life, so the sweet smell of hay can almost make me believe I am home."

A horse neighed, causing a chorus to follow.

"But you're not." I spun on my heel, my headache too painful to deal with more of his relaxed conversation. Talking as though we were friends.

"It's a lot." I ignored him, stepping out of the barn, until he said, "The expectations they have on you." He continued speaking, taking my frozen stance as approval. "You can't be much older than my daughter." His voice cracked. I dug my nails in my palms, wondering why I wasn't leaving. "Life was always hard on her. And the pressure to choose her future was worse because she was always seen as other. Probably not too dissimilar to what it must feel to be a prince?"

I dug my nails deeper, fighting against turning around and snapping that he knew nothing. I breathed in through my nose. Held it. Then released. A technique I had learned to control my emotions around my father.

"Well." I blinked as he spoke again. "I may not understand the weight you carry, but I am a good listener." He started whistling some tune.

My feet were able to move again and I walked away. My mind felt heavy. As though I had drunk as much as I had that one time years ago. A lesson I learned quickly not to repeat. The cold air was doing nothing to fix it.

Yet I kept walking. I kept going until I realized where my feet were leading me.

I stopped under the archway and in the direction of the Healing House. Light emitted from it. Through clenched teeth, I released a muffled roar and kicked some stones from the debris. It was a mistake to come here. A waste of time. I kicked again. And Again. Until my foot ached and I got her little face out of my head. I left, ignoring the desecrated remains around me. With each step, I pulled myself back together, becoming once more the King's Wraith.

CHAPTER 4

Raph

THE FIRST TIME I'D stepped into Alon's study, everything felt different. Better. It was the only place I felt comfortable after I'd agreed to leave the city I'd known all my life. Alon would invite me when he sensed I was struggling, even when I tried to hide it. Later, it became a place of pride, as his summons turned into invitations for more responsibilities, pulling me deeper into his inner circle. A week ago, after we returned from that botched mission, was the first time I'd been called there to be reprimanded.

I stared at his door, stalling, no idea what to expect on the other side. Rolling my shoulders back I tapped my knuckles against it. The door opened, wafting out the familiar sharp smell of ink and melted wax.

"Come in, Raph," Alon said, standing by the far wall with his nose in a book. I longed to ask what he was researching this time, but held my tongue. The pages thumped together as he closed them and turned to his desk.

"I need you on guard duty for tonight's dinner," he said with his back facing me.

I ground my teeth together. He was still punishing me. "Yes, sir," I said, swallowing my pride and accepting my dues.

"Also, plans have shifted." He leaned forward using his hands to brace himself on the desk as he scanned over the papers lying about. "You will be leading a reconnaissance team to Llycia."

I blinked.

He peered up, studying me like a map before sliding a piece of parchment across the desk. It was a list of names.

Adira and Eitan were the first two, along with a handful of others I recognized.

"Sir?" The parchment crinkled slightly in my grip.

He straightened. Behind his desk, he seemed taller. "You will be in charge of the team heading to Llycia." He raised his brow. "I thought you'd be happy about this opportunity...unless you believe someone else might be better for this mission?"

"Yes-no—I'm honored, sir. I only wondered," I glanced back at the list, trying to wrap my head around this sudden change, "when do we depart?"

"As soon as you can get your supplies in order."

"And Nefali? Who will watch over Princess Talia? Her safety—"

"Her safety is *my* concern," he said, the words clipped. Then he sighed. "Remember what this is all for, Raph. This is bigger than you and me. And now, more than ever, we must stay the path."

I hesitated long enough for his eyebrow to lift.

"Will this be a problem?" he asked.

"No, sir." I folded the piece of paper and tucked it behind my back, gripping it too tightly. "I only wondered if Adira and Eitan might take over in protecting Her Highness. She trusts them, which will be beneficial for that mission."

"They will be joining you in Llycia."

A dull weight settled in my gut. "I understand," I answered, even though I didn't.

"Good." Alon picked up a stack of papers from his desk. "You are dismissed."

"Sir, may I ask, why the sudden change? What exactly are you wanting us to uncover in Llycia."

"Due to the storms we've had a lack of communication, more than we're comfortable with. I need someone I can trust on the streets, keeping an eye and ear out for what Madden is doing. And with your connections, you're the best man for the job. Unless you don't feel ready for this?"

I clenched my jaw. "I'm honored, sir. I won't let you down."

"I know," he said, dropping his gaze back to the papers.

My feet remained stuck to their spot. An internal war was raging inside me. Following orders had never been a problem before, but the idea of leaving Talia had my whole body on edge.

He looked back up when he realized I hadn't left. "Make sure you get everything in order. We want your team to leave as soon as possible."

"Yes, sir." I turned on my heels and left.

Voices behind the door grew louder. I shifted my weight and stared straight ahead. The doorknob turned and the voices carried into the once silent hallway.

"Well done, Your Highness," said Hanna holding the door open. "You will be more than ready for your time in Nefali."

"Thank you." Talia dipped her head. "I'm grateful for your wisdom and advice." Her smile stayed on like a mask. It hadn't changed in the past two days–polite, pleasant, and utterly unreadable. But as she stepped away I caught the smallest tremble in her fingers as she clasped them together.

"It's my pleasure." Hanna placed her hand on her heart. "You take after your parents in so many ways. And I dare say, you were born to be a princess."

Talia's smile twitched, a flicker, but it was enough.

"Thank you again, Hanna, but I'd better go. A princess can't be late for her own dinner." Talia fixed her smile and turned, her shoes clicking against the stone floor.

Her eyes widened when she looked straight at me. I parted my lips, but she turned her head and walked past me quickly. Exhaling, I lengthened my stride to catch up to her. I had bribed her new guard to let me escort her to the dinner, hoping to find an opportunity to explain things.

"Please, Talia," I whispered harshly. "I want to explain."

She quickened her steps. "I'm late."

Her rejection stung worse the second time, but I deserved it. The space between us grew, and I studied her from behind. She moved like a statue, with perfect posture, hands folded, head high. But the tension in her shoulders didn't match the grace she wore like armor.

Voices echoed against the stone walls as we approached the dining hall. Two guards stood at the open doors. I slowed, taken by surprise. Alon had been adding guards around Skyhall but it was usually only one or two for events like these. They bowed their heads as Talia walked past them and faintly gestured in my direction as I followed. The room quieted, and everyone stood as Talia walked toward the table full of Aydencian leaders and well-known citizens.

"Good Evening," she addressed the table with a gracious smile. Everyone bowed their heads and returned her greeting.

Another guard was already stationed by the wall closest to the empty chair reserved for Talia. I took my post next to the guard. We acknowledged each other with a nod. Four guards for a simple dinner. My lips pressed together. And Alon didn't trust me enough to have given me a forewarning.

Talia remained standing. For a moment, I thought she meant to stay that way, until Richard hissed someone's name under his breath. The man seated nearest Talia jumped away from his chair, and a screeching filled the room. I launched forward as he moved toward her. He pulled her chair out and she moved around, graciously lowering herself into it.

I regained my composure as everyone else took their seats, and the dinner Richard had arranged began. I scanned every familiar face at the table, searching for any strange behavior or mannerism, but it seemed the only strangeness was coming from our princess.

"Your Highness, I must say you are nothing less than the perfect image of royalty," the man who had pulled out Talia's chair said, leaning toward her. I recognized him as one of Aydencian's prominent business men. I had met him a few times at different occasions but never took the time to remember his name. "Your grandparents, the late king and queen, would be proud."

The man's compliment hung in the air like thick perfume.

Talia gently placed her fork down and picked up her napkin to dab at her mouth as she swallowed. Silverware scraped across plates. A smirk already played at the corner of my mouth as I waited for her reply.

"Thank you. That means ever so much to me." Her voice was smooth and polite, but her fingers twisted the hem of her napkin under the table.

My face slackened.

The man rubbed his hands on his pants. "Our introduction was brief before, and I desperately wanted to talk with you again. I persuaded Richard to place me next to you tonight. I hope you don't mind, Your Highness."

Talia shook her head gently, and his face lit up.

"I didn't have time to share with you before, but I actually grew up in the palace as a child." I released my breath through my nose. "My parents were nobles.

My father was about to join the royal council." The man looked expectantly at Talia.

Her fingers curled around her fork, but her tone stayed even. "How wonderful," she replied, before taking another bite of food.

The man's chest deflated. "Yes, it was," he mumbled to himself, feigning interest in the food on his plate.

Across the table, Richard caught her eye. He didn't smile or frown. He just watched. The break in their conversation opened the door for the woman on Talia's right to strike up a conversation of her own. The rest of the evening was much the same, leaders and ex-nobles vying for her attention. The whole time she kept the same pleasant smile on her face. It was maddening to watch. She was acting like the perfect princess, exactly what Richard and Alon wanted, but it wasn't her. It wasn't Talia.

Richard eventually dismissed everyone, and I followed Talia back to her room. She remained silent the whole way, ignoring my presence and never dropping her newfound posture. I waited for her to turn. To say something or even yell at me. I was right behind her when she paused outside her mother's room. She reached for the handle, but her hand curled into a fist at her side.

"Is everything alright, Princess?" I asked.

"Yes." Her voice sounded far off.

"No, it's not." I stepped in front of her. "What's wrong?"

She backed up and blinked rapidly. "Nothing. And it doesn't matter."

"It does. Something is bothering you. You're different," I said, scanning over her.

"How would you know?" Her words cut deep.

"Ahem." A voice pulled our attention. The guard I had bribed waited a few feet to the side of us. "I'm sorry for the interruption, Your Highness. But I'm here to relieve Raph. Alon has requested for him to get some affairs in order."

My jaw clenched.

"That is no problem at all," she answered with the hollow smile that was getting under my skin. "I was turning in for the night." She dipped her head to the guard and then to me. Her smile never wavered.

An uncomfortable feeling took hold in my chest. Her door closed but I stayed, staring at the wood. Why couldn't I just tell her Alon had ordered me to stay away from her. Ordered me to keep my distance. And I had obeyed, but it was getting harder and harder to.

"Is everything okay?" the guard asked from behind me.

"Yes," I answered, turning to make my way down the hall.

I moved fast, boots smacking stone, breath tight in my chest.

My shoulder hit something hard. "Ow!" I stumbled backward but caught a glimpse of bright blonde hair.

"Whoa." Adira rubbed her own shoulder. "Where are you off to?"

"I was headed to the academy."

"Oh no you don't. You're joining Eitan and me for some drinks." Before I could object, Adira grabbed hold of my sleeve and dragged me toward the door.

The tavern was too loud and the smell of stale ale, damp cloaks, and burnt meat mixed into a single, choking scent. I dodged a glass as it crashed to the ground, but the contents found their way onto my boots.

"Why are we here?" I asked Adira under my breath as she scanned the crowd.

"Because you need to learn how to relax." She waved her hand in the air at Eitan who stood near a small table in the back.

"There are other ways." I stepped around a couple who needed to find a more private place.

"Of course there are, but what's wrong in sharing a drink with some friends." She steered me through the dense crowd to where Eitan stood.

My boots stuck slightly to the floor as I followed.

"He came," Eitan said to Adira with wide eyes. "You came." He looked at me with a wide grin.

"Yes, Let's get this over with so I can leave." I sat and lifted my hand to try and get the attention of a barmaid. Adira and Eitan shared a look and then joined me at the table. I waved both arms in the air when a barmaid seemed to ignore our table intentionally.

"I already ordered a round," Eitan said, fighting back a laugh.

I dropped my arms and fell back into the chair.

"So...rough day?" Adira asked.

"Unexpected," I answered.

"Because of Alon's new mission for us?" she asked, pinning me with a look.

I looked at her and then Eitan. "You know?"

They shared a look. Talia wasn't the only one I'd distanced myself from.

"My father informed me this afternoon," Adira said through pressed lips.

"And she told me after dinner." Eitan shrugged.

Adira tilted her head, watching me. "And you're okay with leaving on this mission...now?"

I avoided her gaze. "Alon said we leave as soon as we're ready."

"That's not what I meant," she pressed.

I rubbed the side of my temple. "I wasn't expecting it. That's all."

Adira leaned back slightly, and her tone softened. "It did come out of nowhere."

"I thought they didn't plan to send anyone else to Llycia until they had Nefali's support," Eitan said, rubbing his chin. "When they could move ahead with dispatching warriors to the villages."

"Plans change," I muttered. But even as I said it, the order gnawed at me. Why now?

"Did Alon mention what the goal of having us in Llycia is?" Eitan asked.

"With the recent storms and lack of communication they want eyes and ears they can trust on the streets."

"That's it?" Adira asked.

I raised a brow at her.

"Don't get me wrong, I understand, but...it seems like a waste of our resources. Couldn't he have sent anyone?"

Eitan leaned closer. "Maybe he'll explain more before we leave. They seem more paranoid about leaks lately. Remember during our last mission he didn't tell any of us the real reason was to search for the lost princess."

I bit the inside of my cheek. Eitan wasn't wrong. But I didn't know if Alon's distrust was in someone leaking information or me.

A barmaid arrived and set three ales on the table in front of us. She walked away, and Adira leaned forward. "I'm not sure what it is, but something seems off with all of this."

"All of what?" I asked.

"The cause. The war. And my father's been...different. Focused. It's like he's become blind to anything else going on around him." Adira picked at a splinter on the table. "Maybe it's because of Gil."

My chest tightened.

Eitan reached over and rested his hand on hers and offered a small, gentle smile. Her hand stilled, though her expression stayed tight.

I wrapped my hand around the nearest mug. "If Alon believes sending us to Llycia is what's best for the cause," my stomach knotted, but I forced the words anyway, "that's what we'll do." Alon had given me a future when I had nothing. I couldn't forget that. Even if I had broken his trust, especially because I had, proving myself and paying dues for my mistakes was the only way forward. I lifted my mug. "To the cause."

They lifted their mugs slowly. "To the cause," they echoed.

We set the mugs down. Around us, chairs scraped and someone shouted over a bad hand of cards, but none of us said anything.

"Who's joining Talia to Nefali?" Eitan asked.

My grip around the mug tightened as I lowered my gaze. "Alon has assigned a guard to escort her."

I could feel them watching me.

"At least Nadav and Hafsa will be there for her," Eitan offered weakly.

Adira studied me over the rim of her mug. "Have you told her you're leaving"

"We're leaving," I corrected, raising a brow. "But no," I mumbled into my mug.

Her gaze sharpened. "Are you still ignoring her?"

"It was Alon's order." My voice dropped low. "Besides, she doesn't want anything to do with me. Not after I failed to save her father and Jules." The words scraped out before I could stop them. "She hasn't forgiven me and I don't blame her."

"Raph..." Eitan's eyes were heavy with pity.

"You have to stop," Adira said, and her tone forced me to look at her. "What happened was not your fault. No one blames you. I don't blame you."

I looked away, unable to accept her words.

"You've been punishing yourself since we got back," Adira pressed. "Obeying Alon without question and ignoring your friends. Talia—"

"I need to go." I stood and left.

The tavern door slammed behind me, muffling the chatter and laughter. I pulled in a breath, but even that felt tight. Shoving my hands into my pockets, I walked away.

"Raph!" My back muscles tightened at the sound of Adira's voice among the chaos spilling out of the tavern. She raced in front of me, and the noises quieted around us as the door closed.

"Let me say this one thing." She swallowed. "One day you'll realize how foolish you've been, and when that day comes, what has been right in front of you this whole time might not be available anymore."

"I...I don't know what you mean."

She sighed. "You do. Just talk to her. Don't miss out on something that might be great because you think you don't dese—" She stopped as a group walked out of the tavern, passing us along their way. Her gaze turned back to me, and she opened her mouth.

"I need to prepare for our mission," I said, stepping past her.

"Raph!" she called after me. I stopped but didn't turn around. "You deserve it."

I continued forward as the voice in my head told me I could never be deserving of something like that.

CHAPTER 5

Talia

I WIPED MY HANDS on my skirts for the third time as muffled conversations from open shop doors and the creak of cart wheels drifted up to where I stood at the top of the hill. The air smelled of fresh bread, warm and comforting. It was still early, but the streets were alive with the first day of blue skies in over a week, though dark clouds loomed on the horizon, warning more rain was coming. I looked out and for a fleeting moment, I wished I could take it in without the weight of my title pressing at my back.

"Watch out!" A voice from below yelled.

A sharp squeak of wood and iron was followed by a cart's abrupt stop. I flinched as the driver barked at a group of children who scattered with a burst of laughter. Their footsteps faded, swallowed by vendors calling out prices and tools clinking behind shop walls. A soft breeze carrying the briny tang of the harbor tugged at the ends of my cloak. I moved toward the shops away from the homes, my assigned bodyguard right on my heels. A strip of white cloth fluttered in a storefront window. A few shops down, another strip was tied to a cart, and a woman nearby had one around her wrist.

"Your Highness."

The voice came from a shop nearby. Mrs. Donner sat on a stool outside a bakery, her gray hair coiled neatly and her hands folded on her lap. Every morning I'd gone on these walks, she'd been there, watching the hustle of the people before her housework called her back.

I smiled and stepped closer. My guard shifted with me.

"Good morning, Mrs. Donner. How's your hip today?"

"Oh, much better, Your Highness." She clutched her shawl. "Your mother's salve has done wonders. I've been able to get much work done around the house."

"I'm happy to hear it. Although, I thought you were supposed to try and rest your hip for a couple days?" I narrowed my eyes with a small smile.

"Ah." Mrs. Donner waved her hand, dismissing me. "I don't have many days left, I plan to make the most of them." Her gaze drifted toward the bustle of the street, her voice turning thoughtful. "Who knows how many days any of us have left."

Her words hung heavier than she likely intended. But with war pressing at the edges of every thought, I couldn't help hearing more in them.

Before I could reply, a chorus of voices cut through.

"Princess Talia!" I winced at the title as a cluster of children barreled into my legs, nearly knocking me over.

"Whoa," I said with a laugh.

"Play with us!"

"Please! We want to play princesses again." A little girl with a freckled face pulled on my skirt.

"No we don't," two little boys said at the same time.

"We want to play warriors." One lifted a stick and the two of them pretended to fight.

"Ahem." My bodyguard faked a cough behind me.

The two little boys lowered their sticks.

"I'm sorry," I told them, crouching a little so my voice matched their height. "I can't play today." Their faces dropped. It nearly broke my heart. "How about tomorrow we go on a treasure hunt?" I asked.

They jumped up and down with excitement.

"I'll take that as a yes. Meet me by the docks this time tomorrow."

They shouted for me not to be late and ran off toward their next big adventure. I watched them go, wondering how long they'd still have the chance to play games if war spread this far. Would they be safe here in Aydencia? Would they lose loved ones or even parents? The doubt inside me stirred to life. War would only bring bloodshed. Were innocent lives worth stopping King Madden?

"They're going to miss you," Mrs. Donner said softly. I blinked at her. "When you leave for Nefali," she explained.

"Oh." I leaned back. "You've heard?"

"It was announced this morning." Her face was unreadable.

My insides twisted. "By chance, have you seen my mother this morning?" I asked, the urgency to find her growing inside me.

Her eyes warmed. "She stopped here earlier, same as you. Always checking on me before heading on. She's sure keeping herself busy."

Busy. Like me. Anything to keep from dwelling too long on Father or Jules.

Mrs. Donner pointed with her chin toward a row of shops further down, around the corner. "She went that way. Likely to Ms. Soriano's, the seamstress."

"Thank you." I smiled and started down the street, weaving through merchants until I reached the corner. My practiced smile slipped back into place as passersby bowed or offered formal greetings. A few sets of eyes seemed to linger a moment too long. Even though Richard had originally *suggested* for me to get out and mingle with the people, I had come to enjoy my time in the city, observing how they lived.

Turning, I nearly collided with a broad chest.

Raph.

He steadied his stance, and I stopped cold.

Neither of us said anything.

My eye caught a letter in his hand. He moved it behind his back.

The bitterness I'd been carrying flared hot again. "Another errand for Alon?"

"What? No. I mean...I'm informing warriors we lea—" Guilt flicked across his face.

"That you leave for Llycia in a few days?" My tone was sharp, clipped. But I couldn't stop the pang low in my chest, a fear I refused to acknowledge.

There was genuine surprise on his face. "You've heard?"

I glanced behind me at my assigned bodyguard who was standing a few feet away, staring at anything but Raph and me.

"Word got around." I crossed my arms.

Raph's mouth pressed thin. "I planned to tell you."

"Right." I ignored the tightness in my chest. All I wanted was to go to Llycia, and now Alon was finally sending a team, and I wasn't going. No, instead Adira, Eitan, and

Raph were leaving without me. "If you don't mind, I have somewhere to be." I stepped past him. "Best of luck."

"Talia," he called out for me.

I quickened my pace, seeing the shop right ahead, but I knew he was closing the distance between us. I didn't want to talk. I could feel my emotions about to break out, and I didn't want to acknowledge how I truly felt about him leaving.

A bell jingled above my head when I opened the door, followed by the swish of fabric moving.

"I'll be right with you." A woman's voice sang from deeper inside.

Raph's hand wrapped around my forearm as he slipped in behind me. "Talia—" his words died.

"Your Highness." Multiple heads turned to look in my direction. "It's Princess Talia."

The room shifted. Bows and murmured greetings rippled through the shop. My pulse jumped, but my smile snapped into place. The ladies' eyes didn't stay on me. Their focus quickly shifted to Raph who quickly dropped his hand. Many of the younger ladies tilted their heads in his direction and batted their eyelashes. One even gave a shy wave.

Raph's face darkened. "I...ahem...will leave you," he muttered, backing out like a chased rabbit.

A ripple of giggles fluttered through the shop. I bit the inside of my cheek to keep from smiling too widely. I relaxed my shoulders and took in my surroundings.

Rolls of fabric were stacked high, their ends spilling over like a waterfall. The space was packed with color. It was nothing like Jasper's stall. There were probably five times the number of fabrics. A rich, dark green fabric caught my eye, and I couldn't help but reach out to feel its texture between my fingers. It was soft yet shiny, and I hadn't seen anything like it.

"You've got great taste, Your Highness."

I jumped back, dropping the fabric. It was the same voice that called out when I walked in. The woman seemed closer to my mother's age, but looked nothing like her. Her hair was piled on top of her head in a messy style, and she wore a long-tailed coat I'd only ever seen men wear before, but it fit her body perfectly, showing off her curves as she walked toward me.

"Do you like it?" she asked whimsically, holding out the hem of her jacket. The coat was composed of many vibrant colors of various fabrics sewn together. Beneath it was a white tunic along with tight dark trousers.

"Yes. I've never seen anything like it."

"Thank you, Your Highness. It's one of my newest creations. And I must say, I'm quite fond of it," she said with a large grin on her tan face. That's when I noticed she had almond eyes, which were similar to Nadav and Hafsa's. "I can make you one, if you'd like."

"Oh, no, Ms—"

"Ms. Soriano, Your Highness."

"It's a pleasure to meet you. I'm actually here looking for my mother."

"Of course." The large smile stayed painted across her face. "Come with me."

I followed her through a velvet curtain into a room with mirrors and a raised platform, then into another space where long wooden tables stretched from one end of the room to the other, each cluttered with vibrant piles of fabric, spools of thread, pin cushions, and half-formed garments. Women worked behind the tables with quiet focus, their fingers moving with practiced speed: snipping, folding, and stitching.

"Here she is, Your Highness," Ms. Soriano said, extending her arm toward the back corner of the room. My mother was bent at the waist, her hands cupping something small, an ointment tin I realized. She spoke in low, warm tones to an older woman seated behind the table.

"Thank you," I said to Ms. Soriano.

"Of course. Your mother has been such a help to our community. We don't know what we would do without her."

I plastered on a smile as I took my leave and headed in my mother's direction.

"Make sure you put this balm on at least twice a day," my mother said, her voice firm but kind. "And try to make sure you take breaks when needed."

It was the voice of my childhood, steady, competent, and comforting. I paused to listen. If I closed my eyes, I could almost imagine I was helping Mother with a home visit. It didn't surprise me that she had already found her place here, but as I watched her, something twisted inside me.

"I will try, Ms. Caffrey. Thank you," the older woman said, taking a tin canister from my mother.

"Very good." My mother straightened and turned around. "Oh, Talia!" she exclaimed, placing a hand over her chest. "Is everything alright?" Her eyes danced over my body and then my surroundings.

"Yes," I said quickly. Then softer, "I thought we could talk."

Her face eased. "Of course. I have deliveries to make. Walk with me?"

I followed her through the shop and back into the street. The morning had warmed, the blue sky still holding despite the dark clouds gathering at the horizon.

As we moved through the bustle, voices called out. "Your Highness." "Princess Talia." Each greeting brushed against me like sandpaper, but I kept my smile in place.

Mother peered at me, lines deepening between her eyes. "Talia," she murmured, lowering her voice so only I could hear, "is this what you want?"

I faltered. "What do you mean?"

Her gaze stayed steady. "All of this. The bowing, the expectations. You don't have to agree to any of this. We can find another way to save your father and Jules."

The memory of our last conversation surfaced. How she wanted me to stay true to myself. It had been four days since then and her words still ate at me. I had no idea who I was.

I swallowed hard. "I agreed to go to Nefali."

She stopped walking and her face tightened. "I've heard."

Guilt soared through me. "I planned to tell you that night, but after everything, I sort of forgot."

She gave a reluctant nod.

"I'm sorry I didn't come sooner," I said.

"I understand." She placed her hand on my shoulder. "I only thought it was time for you to know the truth about that night."

"I'm glad you told me." My throat thickened. "But it was a lot to process. It all has been," I said, blowing out the air in my lungs and along with it the weight I had been carrying about not fixing things with her.

"Is everything okay?" she asked, her concern deepening the corners of her eyes.

"Yes—No..." I guided us into a quieter alley. "I know going to Nefali is the best way I can help Landore and in turn, Father, Jules, and Gil."

"But are you ready for it?"

The question cut deeper than I wanted to admit. My lips parted, but no answer came.

She sighed. "Talia, you don't have to go. Not if it doesn't feel right. You don't have to be the lost princess if it's not the future you want." She squeezed my hand, as if to anchor me. Something I needed more than I realized. "Your father and I never pushed you toward a calling because we wanted you to choose your own future. A choice you can still make."

My throat burned.

"All I want," she said, her eyes searching mine, "is for you to be happy. To live a life that is truly yours."

I swallowed hard, forcing air into my lungs.

Her expression lightened, the heaviness retreating a little. "Dinner tonight. Just us. No formalities, just a mother and her daughter."

Relief loosened my throat. "That sounds perfect."

"Wonderful." She kissed the top of my head, then adjusted the bag at her side. "I have a few more items to drop off, but I'll meet you back at Skyhall later."

I nodded, managing a smile. "I have another lesson with Hanna and Hafsa soon to help prepare me for Nefali."

Her smile faltered slightly. "I'll see you soon."

We parted ways at the end of the alley, her footsteps fading into the crowd. Mine carried me back up the mountain, though my mother's words still pressed against me: *You have a choice.*

CHAPTER 6

Kasper

"YOUR HIGHNESS." A SCOUT pulled up his horse next to me. The endless pounding of hooves against the forest floor and the sway of the horse's gait had transfixed me into a daze.

"Your Highness," he said again, voice low but urgent. "The river has veered west, and there is no sign of any water."

"The closest village?" I asked, tracking the height of the sun.

"Southeast of here. It will take us off course a little, but we'll reach it before sundown."

That was only a few hours away.

"Inform the rider up front," I said. "Scout the village. I don't want any surprises."

"Yes, Your Highness." The scout clicked his tongue, and his horse surged ahead.

Hooves shifted over uneven ground as we veered southeast. Voices rose behind me, questioning. I drowned them out. Focused on the sturdiness of my saddle. The same thing I'd done since we left Hattlee three days ago.

The sun dropped behind the treetops, stretching shadows across the ground. By the time the scout returned, the warmth in the air had vanished.

"We are outside the village's border, Your Highness," he said.

"And the state of the village?" I asked.

"It seems to have been visited by Lieutenant Revel." I tightened my hold on the reins. "However, the village is in a better state than Hattlee, Your Highness."

"Get preparations in order for the horses and have some men stay behind to set up camp. I don't want to spend more time in the village than we have to."

He trotted off, but the sound of hooves remained.

Sal rode up beside me, and his horse fell into step with mine. "The men won't complain if we stop for the night," he said. "A hot meal, some drinks, maybe a few willing locals..."

I kept my eyes ahead. "We ride out at dawn."

"Of course. Still, it wouldn't hurt to let them enjoy a few comforts." He grinned sideways.

"They'll manage."

The trees thinned ahead.

"Is there a rush to get back to Llycia?" Sal asked with a lilt to his voice.

"We ride at dawn," I repeated the order, nudging my horse with my heels.

"You might outrun Revel's report, Your Highness," Sal said, still close, "but don't forget I will be giving my own report when we reach Llycia. The king expects results."

My grip tightened around the leather reins as the tree line finally broke. The village's crude wooden gates came into view. One was half sagging off its hinge like it had given up trying to hold anything back.

Distant shouts echoed from within, too sharp to be trading chatter. I sat straighter. But the closer we rode, the more the tension in my chest eased. People moved among stalls, bartering like one would expect in a penta. Everything looked broken, but the village was functioning.

"Papers!" A guard barked from outside one of the callings' quarters.

She fumbled with a folded slip and handed it over to the guard's waiting hand. He scanned it, nodded, and jerked his chin at the sack in her arms. She opened it. He shoved a hand inside, sifted through what looked like potatoes, then stepped back.

"Proceed."

The woman didn't look up as she moved on.

I scanned the other entrances. It was the same. Guards. Lines. Inspections.

A guard barked and shoved between two villagers from different callings, driving them apart. Those around scattered, keeping their heads low.

Our company stopped outside the village's tavern. I dismounted and allowed one of the men to lead my horse away.

"Prince Kasper!"

My jaw clenched as one of my father's officers strode up full of eagerness.

"An honor, Your Highness." He bowed. "I promise all is still in order since Lieutenant Revel left over a week ago. You can report back to the king we've got patrols at every gate and weekly home raids to keep rebels and rebel sympathizers out." A smug grin took over the officer's face. "There's room at the tavern if—"

I raised my hand. "We're not staying."

His brow twitched, and he opened his mouth to say more.

"I'll inform the king of your...efficiency," I said, stepping away.

"Thank you, Your Highness," he called after me.

Most of the men in my company had scattered to fill their canteens, but a few leaned against the tavern wall. Their expressions were tight as they stared out at the penta crowds. I followed their line of sight to a quarter's entrance where more villagers were being inspected before being let in.

Shifting my focus, I headed toward the stables, but two of the guards caught my eye. They were in charge of the rebels, who were nowhere to be seen. I scanned the area until I found the prisoners tied to a hitching post in front of the neighboring building. They were slumped, wrists bound tight. Even from this distance, I could see the same clenched tension in their faces as the men's.

A small girl with sunkissed brown hair slipped through the crowd and walked toward them, alone. My chest locked up. *Jemma?* Her name caught in my throat before I could stop it.

She crouched beside Jules, her frame almost hidden behind the post. I blinked. The girl placed something over Jules's wrists. I stepped closer. It was a cloth. Carefully, she wiped away the dried blood with slow, gentle strokes.

Jules murmured something. The girl giggled, glancing toward the blond rebel. She still hadn't looked in my direction.

Before I realized it, I'd taken another step closer. Jules's smile vanished. She said something sharp and urgent while struggling against her bindings. The girl spun right into Sal's grip. He yanked her back hard.

A scream ripped through the penta.

"Let her go!" Jules yelled, pulling as hard as she could against the pole.

Sal dragged the girl closer to the tavern. Her face was more narrow and older compared to the one imprinted in my mind. I remained rooted to my spot as her feet skidded against the packed earth. A crowd formed around Sal and the girl. It was a mix of villagers and King's Guard.

"Ana!" A woman ran toward them, but two guards stepped in her way, restraining her.

Sal raised the girl's arms high as if she were a thief he had caught. "Any sign of mercy shown to a rebel will be immediately met with disciplinary actions," Sal yelled, peering out over the crowd.

The girl's toes scraped desperately for balance.

Sal's free hand slapped across her face before releasing his hold on her.

Gasps rippled through the crowd as the girl crumbled to the ground. Jules's screams tore through the penta, filled with rage, helplessness, and guilt. Every muscle in my body coiled. But I didn't move.

Sal faced the crowd with his hand on the pommel of his sword. "This is your only warning. King Madden will not tolerate any form of treason." He scanned the crowd, eyes daring someone to speak.

No one did.

The villagers parted as Sal strode toward the tavern. He glanced my way. One brow lifted, baiting me. A challenge. My teeth slammed together.

A clatter at the village gate pulled my attention to where a group of riders entered, kicking up dust. Oliver rode at the front. He dismounted quickly and made his way to me.

"Camp is set up, Your Highness," he announced.

I grabbed the reins from his hands as Sal's threat burned in the back of my mind. I needed answers. "Bring the blond rebel to my tent," I ordered, swinging myself onto the horse. I spun the horse around and galloped out of the village, but I failed to miss the flash of Jules's tear-streaked face and the glint of fresh blood soaking the ropes at her wrists.

CHAPTER 7

Raph

Sea mist licked at my face. I shifted my weight on the dock's warped boards. The tide slammed steady against the pilings, a mere heartbeat beneath my boots. Behind me, the crowd pressed in. A restless, humming mass held back by rope and guards. I stood with arms crossed, close enough to step in if needed, not that Talia needed me anymore. Not officially.

Her bodyguard loomed behind her, shoulders rigid and his hands poised too close to her waist. He would accompany her to Nefali. She moved toward the edge of the dock, where the rope separated the villagers, her chin high and back straight. Only her fingers betrayed her, tightening behind her back.

The crowd stilled.

"Dear people of Aydencia," she called, voice strong but flattened by memorized lines, "I stand before you, your lost princess—"

Cheers broke out. Fists in the air. Children stomped on crates. An elderly woman dabbed her eyes. And then...

Stillness.

Near the back, wedged between two crates, a hooded man stood unnaturally still. He wasn't watching Talia. His gaze slid past her and the crew to the knarve. Calculating. The man stumbled forward, revealing a white cloth around his forearm. He righted himself and yelled something over his shoulder from where it seemed he had been pushed. I narrowed my eyes and moved forward.

"I stand before you," Talia pressed on, rising over the crowd's dying cheers, "carrying the strength of our cause beyond these borders. What began here is more than survival. Aydencia is a symbol of hope. Hope for a better future." Her smile slipped. "The kingdom of Nefali stands as a potential ally, so I am leaving with the full trust of your leaders to seek support that could secure not only our future but the future of a new Landore."

The crowd roared again.

I looked for the man but couldn't spot him.

Talia let the rest of the speech die on her lips and raised a hand instead. She turned and approached the line of Aydencian leaders who stood between her and the ship. The first leader bowed. Talia paused, giving a half-second glance toward the knarve's gangplank and then further down the line where her mother stood before she refocused on each approaching leader.

One by one they stepped forward, bowed, and offered some words. Most likely empty praises or reassurances. Tipping her head slightly in their direction, Talia plastered a closed smile on her face. Once through the line, she took her first step onto the gangplank and stopped to give one final wave to the people.

The crowd burst into scattered cheers, swelling forward against the ropes. The mooring line groaned under the shifting tide. Talia staggered, catching herself a moment too late. I flinched as her guard's hand reached around her waist to support her.

Heat sparked in my gut, sharp and bitter.

From the corner of my eye, I caught Adira watching me. She and Eitan flanked me.

Talia's eyes scanned the docks until they landed in our direction. She dipped her head toward Adira and Eitan, an actual smile lighting her features.

Finally, her eyes locked on mine.

The noise of the crowd fell away as I kept my gaze solely on her.

The moisture in my mouth evaporated as an urgency to be by her side took hold of me.

She turned away. Her shoulders squared as she took her first step onto the knarve, not looking back.

A cool pinprick tapped my cheek. Then another. Dark clouds had rolled in from the horizon. A sprinkling rain salted the deck and dock.

I looked at Alon and Richard who seemed unfazed by the rain or the darkening clouds moving in. Richard dipped his head at Talia as if encouraging her to keep going. I shifted forward. Were they pushing her departure?

Talia's face was tight, but she quickly buried whatever worry she had and stepped back into the role of princess.

Sailors called out to each other across the deck. They adjusted ropes and tightened the sails. Talia stood facing forward, one hand on the polished wood.

The ropes slipped, and the knarve nosed off the pier. The crowd dispersed, their voices shifting to talk of trade and ration schedules. I didn't move.

Adira touched my shoulder as she murmured something to me. I gave a small acknowledgement but kept my focus on the ship. She and Eitan passed me, their footsteps swallowed by the tide.

A gust of wind rolled off the sea and snapped the sails full.

The knarve jerked once—then again, harder. It veered right, listing too early.

"That's not the wind," Eitan muttered, coming next to me, followed by Adira.

We watched frozen as the vessel pivoted, half-spun, then stalled completely.

"Talia," I breathed out. My feet raced against the wooden boards bringing me closer to the edge of the dock.

The sails were released, while polearms and oars stabbed at the water in frantic rhythm to keep the knarve from veering further. It made an ugly arc toward a lineup of other ships.

Sailors scrambled around me.

Gasps rippled across the docks and led into the crowd that had reformed as the knarve barely missed colliding with another vessel.

Some people cheered, but most looked on unsettled.

The three of us jogged to the dock where the knarve was coasting in.

"Go," I told Adira and Eitan. "Make sure she's okay."

"What about you?" Adira asked.

"I need to check something," I said, letting them pass me and join the chaos ahead.

I scanned the area until I found the port master on duty. He stood at the back of the pier, arms crossed over his belly, posture too relaxed for what was happening around him.

"You," I snapped as I closed the distance. "Who was in charge of inspecting the vessel before departure?"

He gave a slow blink. "Captain Tipper and his crew."

"They cleared it with no issues?"

"Yes."

"Did anyone double-check the rudder line?"

"Not protocol," he said, looking over my shoulder.

I clenched my jaw until it ached.

"She listed." I fired back. "There's a difference between current and structural malfunction." Heat traveled up my neck.

"Accidents happen. Lines break." His brows hitched. Like I was making noise for nothing.

Movement at the edge of my vision pulled me to the end of the dock. Adira and Eitan were with Talia, her guard tight at her shoulder. She looked over and found me across the distance.

Anger and hurt flickered through her eyes before she turned back to Adira. A hollow ache spread through my chest, leaving my breath uneven. My boots shifted forward—

The port master cleared his throat. "Like I said, it probably caught some drag in the tide."

I stared at him, the rain beading in his beard, and swallowed what I wanted to say. This complacency and shrugging off details would get someone killed. Would get *her* killed. I turned on my heel, scanning for Eitan and Adira again. They stood alone, close in conversation.

"She's okay," Adira said as I jogged up. "Alon whisked her straight to Skyhall."

I stopped short. "Alon himself?"

Eitan nodded. "Hauled her off in a frenzy."

I released my breath through my nose. "Check the rudder line."

They exchanged a glance. "The rudder line?" Adira asked. "Why?"

I looked between them, voice low but firm, "Something's off."

"You think it was deliberate?" Eitan's eyes widened.

"I don't know. But I'm going to find out." I stepped back. "Check the line yourselves."

They nodded as I turned toward Skyhall.

The door slammed shut.

I exhaled a sharp groan and ran a hand down my face and began stripping off the scabbard across my chest. I tossed it onto the bed. A few of the knives clattered after it, dull thuds against the thin blanket. My sleeves were pushed back, but I rolled them higher.

Cold water hit my skin like a slap. I braced myself over the basin, arms locked, shoulders tight. Droplets slid from my brow, dripping into the pool below.

Why is he ignoring the evidence?

I grabbed a towel nearby and wiped my face.

He didn't even flinch when he lied to me about it. "Frayed rope," he'd said. Nothing more than a simple accident. But the rope wasn't just frayed, it had also been cut.

A growl ripped from my throat as I hurled the towel across the room. It hit the wall and fell limp, useless. Much like Alon's excuses. I stared at the door. The light off the full moon cast dark shadows across it. My breath was short.

Inventory. Like a first-year. After I'd brought him evidence, after I'd begged him to listen. He punished me with errands. Pushing me aside and withholding the truth. I was done with it all.

I shoved open the door and stepped into the corridor, leaving behind my knives and whatever sense I had left. I skidded on the stone, barely avoiding a collision with two of Alon's guards rounding the corner into the men's wing. Their eyes were half-lidded, either from exhaustion or boredom. I threw up a hand and nodded a silent apology as I passed but didn't slow down.

Around the corner, the main hallway was empty. I stepped out as a familiar voice hit my ears. "Yes, today was unfortunate, but it was an accident. We can have another ship ready for the morning." My heart hammered against my chest.

With silent steps, I followed Richard's voice down the hall.

"There is no rush, sir," Hafsa said as I came to a door cracked open. I leaned closer, breath shallow. "Our king and queen would demand the princess's safety comes first. Plus, they will take all the time we can give them to prepare for her arrival."

"I'm sure they have much to prepare for," Richard replied.

"Are you sure it's the wisest decision not to inform Her Highness of the arrangement that has been made?" I pulled back at the closeness of Nadav's voice.

"We can't afford for her to object," Richard answered, and at the same time, my boot scuffed against the stone floor.

I froze.

No one spoke.

Heat flared at the back of my neck.

"As you wish, sir," Nadav said.

I breathed and silently stepped away from the door.

"We need to make sure she gets on that ship." Richard's voice was a whisper as I distanced myself.

I stalked down the hall. My fists curled at my sides, nails biting into my palms. Secrets stacked upon secrets. I couldn't ignore it anymore. Alon dismissing the obvious sabotage. Richard scheming in the shadows. And Nadav and Hafsa...

The people I was supposed to trust most were building walls of secrets around me. Around her. They were hiding something, and I was ready to rip it wide open.

Chapter 8

Talia

Rain drummed faintly overhead, muffled by the stone but steady enough to sink into the mountain. Skyhall felt smaller on wet days. The candles flickered low, their flames pressed flat, their glow swallowed by damp tapestries. Hanna's lesson room always felt smaller on days like this, the air thick enough to taste.

Hafsa sat opposite me at the narrow table, back straight, hands calm. Even though she had hardly spoken, her presence filled the space. Hanna stood between us, unable to keep still.

"At least the rain gives us time," Hanna said, smoothing the front of her dress and then rearranging the papers in front of her. "Your departure can wait until it clears and we can prepare you properly. My husband forgets training like this takes years." The smile she offered me was kind, but her eyes carried shadows too deep to hide. "We'll do what we can."

"About the ship," I asked, still able to feel the fear that overtook me yesterday on the vessel when it went out of control. "Is there any more news?"

They looked at each other quickly. Hafsa's gaze was the first to return, but Hanna spoke. "Didn't Alon already share that the rudder line had unfortunately frayed enough to have snapped?"

"He did." I bit my lower lip.

"Those things do happen from time to time," Hanna said, repeating the same exact words Alon told me, but there was something about it all that rubbed me wrong. A feeling that poked at the back of my mind. There was more to it all. Or why did Alon rush me to Skyhall as if I was in danger?

"Now," Hanna clapped her hands, "posture."

I lifted my chin as Hanna circled me, her hands clasped behind her back. "When you arrive in Nefali, you'll be seated before the king and queen. At this moment, negotiations have begun. They won't ask you anything about them at this point, but they will be watching your every move, judging you."

"But I thought negotiations had already been made through Alon and Richard?" I asked, unable to stop the crease between my brows from forming.

"Yes, for the war, but it all hinges on their request to meet you in person." Hanna's words brought a chill down my spine.

"Show them respect," Hafsa added, her tone steady. "Honor is their foundation. Bow too shallow and you offend. Bow too deeply and you make yourself lesser." I snatched the quill in front of me and tried to jot down her words before they slipped away. "They will listen closely to the weight of your silence as much as your words. Pause before you answer. Choose your words sparingly. They will respect restraint."

"So basically pretend I'm you," I mumbled, stretching out the cramp in my hand. A small smile lit Hafsa's face.

Hanna spoke, not seeming to have heard me. "You will be invited to many gatherings and each one of these will be a test. Your guard can never drop. You must be a princess at all times, you never know who will be watching."

My shoulders sagged against the chair. I wasn't a diplomat. I wasn't raised for this. I was raised as a simple village girl. What right did I have to sit across from another kingdom's king and queen and speak for Landore?

My voice cracked before I could stop it. "How am I supposed to do this? What if I—"

"You will not fail," Hanna said quickly, her tone sharp. She came to stand in front of me. "You know what is at stake. This isn't only about gaining their support.

This is about Gil. About your father. About Jules." The names landed like stones in my chest. "You carry the hope of a better future." Her hand hovered near my arm, trembling faintly before she pulled it back. "You will not fail," she repeated, but it seemed more to herself.

Guilt clenched tightly around my throat. I sat on my hands, trying to still them.

Hafsa leaned forward slightly, her eyes searching mine. "You won't be alone. And remember, they too want this treaty to work. You are not powerless." Her words grounded me for the briefest moment. I nodded, though everything felt too tight: my clothes, the room.

"Let's practice," Hanna said briskly. She drew her shoulders back, her voice suddenly regal, carrying the weight of a kingdom. "Why should Nefali risk war by allying with Landore against their own king?"

I swallowed, my voice uneven at first. "Because doing nothing will cost you more. King Madden's reign has not only hurt Landore, it's poisoned all the kingdoms."

Hanna moved forward, assessing. "And what do you offer in return for our support?"

I sat straighter, forcing the words out like memorized lines. "We offer unity, open borders, and renewed trade between our kingdoms. Along with restoration of safe passage where ships have been seized and goods stolen under Madden's reign."

Hafsa inclined her head slightly. "Better to frame it as partnership. Do not place them above you. You are their equal. Say: 'Together, we will reestablish the flow of goods and culture between our kingdoms. Together, we will open what Madden closed.'"

I repeated the words under my breath. They landed heavy on my tongue, too large for me, as if I were wearing someone else's voice.

A rap struck the door.

"Enter," Hanna called.

The hinges groaned as the door opened, revealing Raph with damp hair and shadows hollowing his eyes. He inclined his head toward Hanna, Hafsa, and then me. His eyes lingered on Hafsa for a brief second before looking back at Hanna. "You and Hafsa are requested for a council meeting."

Hanna's mouth tightened. "Now?"

He nodded once.

Hanna gathered the papers on the table in her arms, mumbling something under her breath. "We will continue this later." She bent toward me, her voice quiet. "Remember this is for them." She straightened and briskly walked out of the room. Hafsa followed but paused at the door, dipping her head toward me before she, too, left.

The silence pressed in as Raph lingered by the door. He stood tall and unmoving, shadows carved deep beneath his eyes. He looked like he hadn't slept.

"Another errand for Alon, I see," I said, pushing from my chair, my tone sharper than I meant.

His jaw tightened. "He needed a message delivered."

"Of course he did." I remained by the table, refusing to move closer until he left, but he continued to stare at me. Heat erupted in the pit of my stomach. "When do you leave?" I quickly asked.

He shrugged. "Whenever the rain clears."

"Has there been any news about Gil, Jules, and my father?"

His face remained blank. "No."

"Well, then." I gestured toward the door he blocked. "I'd like to return to my room."

His feet remained planted.

"Raph, move." I stepped forward.

His face finally cracked, revealing some sort of conflict inside of him.

"I said move!"

"No," he said softly.

"What do you mean, no?" I crossed my arms. "What do you want? Is it another message from Alon? Because if it is, just spit it out."

He shook his head.

"I don't have time for this. If you have nothing to say then move. Or...I'll scream."

His shoulders stiffened. Then, as if ripped from him, the words came. "It wasn't my choice to stay away. It was his order."

My thoughts froze. "What?"

"Alon. After we got back, he ordered me to keep my distance from you. It was my punishment."

His admission cut sharper than I expected and left me angrier. "And you obeyed him. Like always."

"Talia, I tried to. But—"

"Just admit it. No matter what the cost is or who it hurts, you will always obey."

"That's not true." He stepped forward, eyes fierce despite the weariness shadowing them.

"Really?" My pulse hammered. "Prove it."

The air between us thinned. Finally, his voice broke through, rough and gravelly. "Whenever it comes to you, I lose control. I know what I should do but I end up doing the exact opposite. When you ran back into the kidnapper's camp, I knew I shouldn't follow you without backup, but I couldn't help myself. When Jules told us you'd been taken by King's Guards and brought to Llycia, I knew interfering would wreck my mission, but you'd plagued my mind every moment since I last saw you, and I couldn't do nothing." He paused.

My breath faltered. "I don't understand."

He rubbed the back of his neck. "When it comes to you, I can't think straight. All my training and control flies out the window. Even last night, I didn't sleep. I couldn't. Not after what I overheard Richard, Hafsa, and Nadav say about you."

His words punched me in the gut. "What did they say?" His face went white. "Tell me," I demanded.

"They've made some arrangement with the king and queen of Nefali they don't want you to know about."

The room tilted. "An arrangement?"

"I don't know the details. But whatever it is, it means they don't trust you." His hands curled into fists. "I also think Alon is hiding something. He's ignoring the fact the rudder line wasn't frayed, it was sliced halfway through."

I took a few steps back, mind spinning and breath jagged. "You mean, someone cut it *intentionally*?"

"It looks that way." His hand dragged through his hair.

"Why? And why wouldn't Alon tell me?"

"I don't know." He dropped his hand to his side. "I tried to confront him, but he dismissed me. Even after Eitan and Adira relayed their findings about the rope, he called us paranoid. 'Aydencia's safe,' he said. As if the knarve they sent you on hadn't been sabotaged." Anger coated his words.

"So you don't agree?"

Our eyes met. "No. I don't. Something is going on. I just don't know what it is."

I rubbed my arms. "Something with the white cloths? There were more of them yesterday."

His mouth pressed thin, then he exhaled. "Don't go to Nefali. It's not safe, and I can't protect you there."

"What?"

He remained silent for a moment. "Do you want this life?" he asked.

I lowered my gaze.

He stepped closer, voice tight. "Endless dinners. Endless bows. Everyone using you to climb higher. Is that the life you want?"

My head snapped up. "You think I don't know every bow I get is a transaction? Every glance. Every smile. It's all a game. But I—" I tightened my arms around myself. "I... I don't know."

"Talia." He took a step closer to me. "I barely recognize you anymore. You've buried the real you. But," he took three more steps, "I need to know, is this the life you want?"

"Raph..." I stepped back, hands raised. "What do you want me to say? I've changed. Who wouldn't, after everything?"

He stepped back too.

My voice softened. "What I want doesn't matter. I tried that. People got hurt. If hiding some of myself will save those I love, then yes, this is the life I want."

"But you're not safe."

"You don't know that."

"Don't go," he said, his eyes pleading with me.

"What else am I supposed to do?" I clutched the pendant around my neck. "I-I can't run from this. Not after last time."

"That decision," his voice cracked, "plagues me every time I look at you."

"It wasn't *your* fault."

"I was in charge. I made the call. It was my fault, and I'll continue to try to make it right." I could feel the guilt pour off him.

I waited until he looked me in the eye. "I don't blame you. I never have."

Our gazes remained fixed on one another. My cheeks flushed.

"You won't be safe in Nefali," he said, breaking the moment.

"You don't know that." I dug my fingers into my trousers, trying to stay strong. "I have to go. It's where I can make the most impact. But I won't walk into anything blind. We need to figure out whatever it is they're hiding from me."

His eyes searched mine, doubt warring with re-solve. "Okay," he agreed, but bit his lower lip. "All night I've been trying to come up with a plan.

"What if we approach Nadav and Hafsa and ask them outright what is going on?" I offered.

"But how would we know they're telling the truth?"

I pressed my lips together.

"I want to believe they are on our side," he began to pace the small room, "but they're Nèfalese. Their loyalty lies with their kingdom."

"Would anyone else know that we could trust?"

"I...I don't think so."

"What do we do then?" Despair escaped with my words.

Raph placed his fist to his chin, thinking. "I'll break into Alon's study. There has to be some sort of cor-respondence with the king and queen."

"Okay." A spark of hope flared. "When?"

"Alon rarely leaves it. He's known to sleep in there at times." He stopped pacing. "The gathering of war-riors," he said, mainly to himself.

"The what?"

"The gathering of warriors. It's a mandatory gathering for every Aydencian warrior. It happens once a moon cycle and is a time to report about the progress that has been made from those who are undercover in Landore.

It's meant to help build morale and remind us why we do what we do."

"And how will that help us break into Alon's study?"

A smirk pulled at the side of his mouth. "Because it's in two days and Alon helps lead it, which means his study will be vacant."

"Do we have that much time? I thought they wanted me on a ship tomorrow?"

He shook his head. "I don't think Richard and Alon are on the same page about that. Alon told me they were going to delay your departure until things settled down. I'll talk to him again, though."

"Okay, so during this gathering we will break into Alon's study?"

Raph's face went slack.

"What?" I asked.

"I'll be expected to make an appearance. It's manda-tory," he said, already resuming his pacing.

"I can do it alone."

His steps halted and his eyebrows lifted.

"I can do it," I repeated.

"Tal—"

"Please," I said, stepping closer. "It's my life they're planning. Let me uncover the truth."

He hesitated. "Do you know how to pick a lock?"

"No, I admitted, "but I know someone who does."

"What if you get caught?"

"I'll make up an excuse. Who'd believe I'd intentionally break into Alon's study?"

His nostrils flared, and he exhaled hard. "Fine."

Relief surged through me. A smile broke across my face.

But Raph's face didn't match my feelings. His eyes lingered on me with something heavier. "The gathering starts an hour before sunset. Most of Skyhall will be empty, but Alon will have guards positioned around, including your bodyguard…"

"We'll figure something out. I could make a sleeping tonic," I said, not willing to back down. I could do this.

"Let me speak with Adira and Eitan, but that might be our best option."

I nodded as I rocked to the balls of my feet.

His jaw tightened. "I shouldn't let you do this."

"And yet you will."

Silence pulsed between us. He shook his head, half in defeat, half in something else I couldn't name.

"All right," he said at last, voice rough. "But if anything happens—"

"It won't," I cut him off, "I won't fail." I repeated the same words Hanna had said to me, but this time I actually believed them.

CHAPTER 9

Jules

I AWOKE WITH A start. Someone was approaching. It was dark, but I could see two figures coming my way. One was limping. I sucked in a breath and pressed my back against the bark of the tree.

Gil.

The guard tied him to the tree nearest to mine, an arm's length away. My fingers stretched, desperate to reach him. Gil's face twisted in pain as the guard secured his bindings, and he wouldn't look at me.

I opened my mouth to say something the moment the guard was far enough away, but fell short. There was nothing I could do to make any of this go away. Gil was the one he interrogated every night. Gil had the information he wanted, not me. Hopelessness and anger swirled inside me.

"Raph was always the 'suffer in silence' type," Gil croaked. I squeezed my eyes shut. Never thought I would cry with relief at hearing him talk. "And to be honest," he continued, "I still don't get the appeal. This bites." He tried to laugh, but it turned into a wet cough.

"What are we going to do?"

"Grin and bear it?" he replied with a lopsided grin.

"I'm serious," I snapped, louder than I meant to. "That little girl in that village, she—" My voice broke and my breath caught like I'd swallowed gravel. It had been two days, but her face was seared into my mind. "She didn't even do anything," I said, shaking my head. "I sat there and just watched." Shame twisted in my chest. "We can't keep doing nothing. And these nightly interrogations—"

"I can handle it," Gil said. He tried pressing into the ground to lift himself higher. A moan escaped his lips, and he slumped back down. "Plus, tonight was different."

"What do you mean?"

"Kasper was different. Don't get me wrong, he still knew how to throw a mean punch." Gil rubbed his side. "But he didn't demand me to tell him where the rebels were located like usual. I don't know. He seemed sad or something. But I could be wrong. Maybe he hit my head enough times that I'm imagining things."

I leveled Gil with a look of disbelief.

"If I'm not seeing things, I think it could be possible to turn Kasper against his father."

"You're serious?" A laugh almost broke out of me. "You think the King's Wraith would turn against his father, the king, and join us? Gil, that's insane. He would never. You know the things he has done." My eyes flicked to the scar on his face, which was outlined in dried blood. "It will never happen."

Gil didn't say anything as he looked at his bindings.

"We're almost to Llycia," I said, lowering my voice more. "I overheard a couple guards say they believe we will arrive tomorrow."

"We still have a chance. And maybe that chance is being taken to the palace," he said.

My eyes widened.

"Hear me out. If we are in the palace, we might be able to get more information on what is going on. We can work from the inside until a rescue team comes." My mouth pulled tight, lips pressing into a line. "We got Talia out once. They'll find a way to save us."

"Gil—"

"Shut up!" A deep voice growled. The guard's footsteps faded.

I pressed my lips together and stared at Gil. He gave me a tight smile.

My stomach sank. Our chances of escape would be nonexistent once we got behind those palace doors.

Around us, the fire crackled low and the sounds of sleep filled the air. I sat, unable to envision being able to sleep. Gil was slumped against the tree. He didn't speak again, but his words echoed in my head louder amid the silence. *He believed we could turn the prince.*

I wasn't sure what terrified me more: that he was wrong or that he might be right.

Dawn bled slowly through the trees, painting everything in a sickly gray. The camp stirred to life with low grunts and the dull clank of metal. Saddles creaked and boots shuffled over roots. The guards moved stiffly, their words clipped and minimal. No jokes. No bets. Just orders barked through clenched jaws.

My usual guard approached, boots crunching against the brittle ground. He jerked my arms up, and the blood rushed painfully back into my fingers. Across from me, Gil staggered as his guard hauled him upright. He hissed through his teeth before catching himself and straightening.

The ropes rubbed my skin as the guard tied me behind his horse again.

And the march began.

The King's Wraith rode up front, a dark silhouette against the rising sun. From where I trudged, I could only make out the back of his head and the ramrod line of his spine. He didn't scan the tree line, didn't issue a single command.

A younger guard's rein slipped and his horse brushed too closely to the Wraith's mount. The guard sputtered something, grabbing back the reins.

The King's Wraith didn't react.

The thought Gil had planted the night before stirred again, curling uncomfortably in my gut. Ahead, the trees parted, and my body tightened for a whole other reason.

The spires of Llycia speared the sky in the distance, towering over everything, gold-capped and gleaming. The guards straightened in their saddles as we passed beneath the outer gates. The road narrowed, hooves echoed louder, and the voices of Merchants intensified.

Many villagers whispered behind their hands while others openly stared, eyes full of questions as the company snaked us through the winding city. Step by step conversations quieted and heads turned to follow us. I tried to focus on the horse in front of me. To ignore their stares, but it was impossible. A mother yanked her child off the street with wide eyes. A merchant paused mid-call, the apple in his hand forgotten. My bindings chafed, but I forced my face to remain neutral with my chin lifted. I had nothing to be ashamed of.

The dirt street turned to cobblestones, and the alabaster palace rose ahead of us. The iron gates screamed in protest as they opened. My heart hammered against my chest at the palace that stood behind them. Its glow against the descending sun was deceptive, for it was nothing more than a prison.

A chorus of whinnies filled the air, and my rope was tugged forward. I barely kept myself from toppling over from exhaustion. Parading us through the streets of Llycia as obvious prisoners had been intentional.

"Halt," the King's Wraith ordered from ahead.

I looked at Gil. He shrugged.

The guard on my horse dismounted and untied my rope from the saddle. "Move," he said, pulling me. Gil was led by a guard next to me while two others flanked us. Talia's father was in front, untied and directly behind the King's Wraith.

I barely registered our surroundings as they led us through the doors into the palace, though a chill crawled up my spine the further we walked. The raw skin around my wrists burned, and I unintentionally slowed my steps.

Gil lightly nudged my shoulder with his. He gave me a slight smile and a signature wink. It was completely out of place, but it was exactly what I needed.

Whatever sound the double doors had muffled exploded upon their opening. However, the noise within cut off so sharply it left the silence ringing. The hall was full. One hundred people, at least, parted to create an aisle leading to King Madden. The massive room felt bare, cold, and haunting.

Ladies whispered to one another. Their silks shimmered and jewels glinted in the light. They looked calm, refined, hands folded or clasped before them. But the way their lips curved, too eager and too sharp, reminded me of a wolf about to attack its prey. One of them, with dark brown hair and full red lips, looked me in the eye. Her face twisted with disgust.

King Madden remained on his throne. His eyes were small and dark like wet pebbles that watched our every step while his fingers drummed slowly on the armrest. We came to a stop and my knees buckled, finally giving out. I was falling.

Gil's body pressed against mine, keeping me upright. For a beat a hollow certainty slid over my skin, this was how it ends. My vision blurred, but I blinked the unshed tears away.

"Father," the King's Wraith said, stepping forward and into a kneel.

King Madden tilted his head—not in affection, but assessment, like he was wondering how far his son could bend before he snapped.

"I see you have not returned empty handed," King Madden said.

"No, my king." the Wraith stood. "The rebels were holding him captive." He gestured toward John, who was unbound but with two guards directly behind him. "The man who raised Princess Talia."

A small chorus of gasps bounced around the room, followed by whispers.

"Sir," King Madden said, directed at John. "I can't imagine what you've endured. I assure you, I will reunite you with your daughter." The smile he offered was too slow, too practiced. "Please escort him to a room to be cleaned and made comfortable," he added with a flick of his fingers.

The guards ushered John away. I took a step toward them.

"Don't," Gil whispered.

I was forced to watch John limp away as I failed, yet again, at protecting him.

"And these two?" The king's attention shifted to us. The civility in his face dropped, and his expression twisted as if he smelled something unpleasant.

"They were a part of the rebel group that had Princess Talia's father hostage," the Wraith answered.

Madden's gaze cut into me. "The same rebels who kidnapped our dear princess?"

"Yes, Your Majesty."

The whispers around us grew louder again.

"And what of Princess Talia?"

The King's Wraith paused for a moment. "She is still in the hands of the rebels."

King Madden clicked the roof of his mouth. "I can't even imagine what evils they are carrying out on our poor princess."

I pulled against my restraints. This was utter garbage. Every single word that came out of his mouth was a lie.

"Lock them up," someone yelled out.

"Tell us where the princess is!"

"Kill them!"

I looked at Gil. He didn't seem phased. His gaze was on the King's Wraith.

The king didn't shout. He didn't raise a hand. But the room silenced when he stood.

"Do not fear," he said, low and calm. "These two will answer for the crimes the rebels have committed." His hand gently wrapped around the hilt of his sheathed sword.

"My king." the King's Wraith said quickly, cutting through the nobles' hungry stares. "They might be of some use to our efforts in locating the rebel camp."

The king held his smile, though it appeared strained as he said, loud enough for the crowd, "We will get everything we need out of them. Because we will get our princess back."

They clapped their agreement.

"Take them to the dungeon," King Madden ordered.

A tug on the rope yanked me down, and my knees cracked against stone. Laughter echoed like thunder as I tried to stand. I affixed my stare to Gil's back as they led us toward the doors.

How could they be so blind? How could they support him?

The doors shut. The sound cut off, leaving only the scrape of boots and the beat of my pulse. The guards dragged us through the palace, down a set of stairs, and to a familiar door. My breath hitched. It was the same prison cell they had held the young, kidnapped women hostage. Without a single word, they untied my ropes and shoved me into the cell. The door slammed behind me.

Realization hit at the same moment another door slammed shut.

"Jules. Jules." Gil's voice came from the other side of the stone wall.

"Gil," I said as the corner of my eyes tickled with tears.

"It will be okay." I followed his voice where a small gap in two stones was located. I tried to look through it but couldn't see anything. "I promise. I won't let anything happen to you."

I lowered myself to the ground slowly, letting the tears escape freely.

"Don't make promises you can't keep," I whispered, too tired to fight.

"Then I'll keep it," he replied like he believed it enough for both of us.

CHAPTER 10

Kasper

MY FATHER TILTED HIS head until a crack split the air, then straightened to his full height. "Silence!"

The courtiers' voices died in a hush.

"Beyond the safety of our beloved city, the rebels wreak havoc. They have destroyed our villages. Harmed our innocents. And their path is pointed straight for Llycia."

Gasps broke out, sharp and fluttering, like birds startled from cover yet too foolish to flee far from the incoming danger.

"These rebels are a plague we must vanquish. And the only way we can do that is by staying faithful. I ask you, my loyal friends, to stay vigilant. To watch your neighbors, your friends, your servants, for even a breath of disloyalty. If you are caught hiding such rebels, you risk your own life." His hand rested lightly on his sword hilt, a purposeful move.

Everyone remained silent with careful eyes on my father. He sank onto his throne and gave a sharp nod. The rear doors groaned open, and guards swept into the room, ushering courtiers out like livestock.

Celeste paused in front of me, offering a coy smile and a fluttering wave. I turned back toward the dais and waited. Their voices faded down the hall, but my father kept his tense gaze on the doors until it was silent.

"You are all dismissed," he said to the remaining guards.

His thumb tapped a steady rhythm against the throne's armrest, waiting until the doors thudded shut.

His gaze flicked to me. "They're still here," he said, low, certain. "The rebels. In these very walls. Taking Talia wasn't enough." His knuckles whitened on the chair. "They are like rats, burrowing deeper, spreading their plague unseen. And I need you to exterminate them before they strike again."

"Sir?"

"The villagers are beginning to speak back. Lieutenant Revel's last report spoke of a village that called my men murderers. Saying it was them who were burning homes, not the rebels." His jaw clicked as if biting down on the words. "Someone is feeding them this poison. Turning my people against me from within." He let the words land hard.

"How do you know it's coming from within?" I asked.

His nostrils flared. "There are whispers that some in my inner circle are questioning my decisions. And because I know someone aided that rebel in escaping with Talia. They knew of the secret passageway." His hand flexed against the throne's armrest.

"What secret passageway?" I asked. Sal had re-marked after I awoke from the sleeping tonic that Princess Talia and the rebels had used gunpowder to blast their way out of the palace, but he failed to mention a hidden exit.

He frowned and muttered more or less to himself, "No one but myself..." His eyes darted to the right. "Unless..."

"Unless?"

Whatever had captured my father vanished. His sharp gaze locked onto me again. "There are spies inside these walls. I tried to root them out while you were away, but I don't know how deep the betrayal runs. No one is above suspicion." His head jerked toward the side door.

I looked.

Nothing.

There was something he wasn't telling me. He'd han-dled spies before, but this was different. "We need to dispose of those prisoners. I won't have rebel filth rotting under my roof."

"Of course, sir, but, if I may, they could still be useful," I said as my pulse quickened.

"And why is that?"

"One of them is very important to the princess—"

"Keep that one. Kill the other," he said with a flick of his wrist.

"I could. Though the other has shown some promise that he may know the location of the rebels."

"And you haven't gotten it yet?"

"I'm close."

"Kill them," he ordered. "They won't give it up. We need to focus our efforts on finding the spies, not creating more."

Frantically, I worked on finding a solution that would please my father. He was too paranoid to think straight. "What if we turn them into bait?"

He lifted an eyebrow.

"If there are spies in the palace, they'll either try to break the rebels out or make contact. Either way, we can use the prisoners to smoke them out."

His eyebrows pinched together and he rubbed his chin.

"You have a week. Find the spies *and* the location of the rebel camp. Interrogate the father as well. He raised Talia, he knows her weaknesses. When we have her again, we will use them to break her beyond repair." He whipped his head toward the door closest to us where a muffled noise had come from. "Start with the servants," he went on, voice shifting fast. "Question them, watch them, bleed them if you must. One of them knows something about the spies."

Interrogate. Investigate. Exterminate. The pressure in my chest swelled, making it hard to breathe.

My father tilted his head, studying me. "Is this too much for you, boy?" I wiped any emotion from my face. "Perhaps Lieutenant Revel's letter carries some truth. Maybe you are going soft." His gaze narrowed, and my throat dried. "If you fail me..." He leaned forward. "Let's just say, I'm getting tired of keeping your little pet."

White-hot rage tore through me. I clenched my jaw before the tremor could reach it. Blood pounded in my ears. I bowed my head to hide the fury clawing up at me, forcing myself still, locked behind the mask he taught me to wear. "I won't fail you," I said in a trance.

"You're dismissed," he said it casually, but there was a small gleam in his eyes.

The doors shut behind me with a resounding thud. It wasn't enough. Capturing the rebels wasn't enough. None of it was enough to save her.

My fists balled at my sides. The air in the corridor felt too thin, like I was breathing through cloth. The heat in my chest had nowhere to go. And it was searching for something to burn.

"Your Highness," one of the guards stationed in the dungeon said, offering a sloppy bow. "The rebels are in the far cells on the right," he said, unsure of himself.

His face wasn't familiar. But with the call to the villagers for more King's Guards, I wasn't surprised at not knowing him.

He fumbled the keys. "Would you like me to open the door for you?"

"No," I snatched the keys from his hand.

The guard shifted uncomfortably.

"Are there any other prisoners?"

"No, sir. Although one was moved this morning. You will have the whole dungeon to yourself for interrogations," he answered with a pleased look on his face.

I didn't answer. Just turned on my heel as my breath snagged.

That gleam in my father's eye...

I stopped in front of the prison door. I punched the wood. Pain shot up my arm. The sound rattled down the corridor.

Footsteps approached. Thrusting the key into the door, I flung it open and stormed in.

The blond rebel was slumped against the wall. His eyes bore into me, but he didn't move.

I lunged.

"Stand up."

Nothing.

"I said, stand up!" I kicked him in the stomach.

He doubled over with a grunt and didn't get up. I yanked him up by his tunic, and my fist connected with his jaw. The first strike landed hard. He staggered. My second hit connected with the side of his face.

I slammed him into the wall and crushed my forearm against his chest. "Where is it?" I shouted. My voice came out feral. "Tell me!" I delivered a punch to his stomach.

He bent forward, coughing.

"Stop! Please! Stop this!" Jules's voice rang from the next cell, distant and muffled. But my father's words were a knife at my throat and Lliana's face filled every empty space in me.

Another punch. My knuckles screamed. "Tell me where they hole up. How they move. How they knew about the passageway." The rebel's knees gave, and I kept him upright by slamming him against the wall again.

"Kasper, please!" Jules's words matched my desperation, but they couldn't reach me.

"Tell me!" A crunch let out. His nose sprayed blood across my hand.

He clutched his face and then reached out for the wall as he crumpled. Blood smeared against the stone. I stepped back. My breath came in ragged bursts. The cell was too small. The walls were too close. I stumbled out, and the door clanged shut behind me. I fell against the wall, collapsing to my knees. My hands braced against the cold stone, knuckles split and stinging. I couldn't catch my breath.

"One week," I muttered, my voice tight. "I can do this. I have to do this." My forehead hit the wall. I didn't pull it back.

"What happened?" Jules's voice floated from under her cell door.

I looked at the floor. Blood slicked the keys still clutched in my hand. "Nothing," I snapped, then pushed off the floor and walked away.

CHAPTER 11

Talia

SOMETHING SHIFTED IN THE dark behind me. A shuffle, faint, but enough to send my pulse racing. I spun, heart in my throat. The hall was empty. Just shadows. I forced a breath and turned back to the door.

Pick the lock, find the list, and get out. Easy. But a lump formed in my throat as I stood in front of Alon's study.

The keyhole stared at me like a cold, unblinking eye. Adira's two hour lesson ran through my mind, yet the tools felt foreign in my hand. I wiped my palms against my trousers, but sweat still slicked my grip.

First, the tension tool, a piece of thin, bent metal. I slid it in and pushed upward. Next, the hook. I bit my lip and fumbled as I searched for the lever. On my bedroom door it was near the front, but here? Nothing. Sweat dripped from the nape of my neck, and my fingers slipped on the tools.

I yanked them out, and my chest clenched. The hallway remained silent, but the feeling someone could round the corner at any second traveled up my spine.

A small gasp left my mouth. I'd been working from the wrong side. A glimmer of hope gave me some relief as I placed the first tool back in. With the second tool, I pushed it further to the back before lifting it to feel for the lever.

Click.

I exhaled.

I slipped into the study and closed the door behind me. It was completely dark. No windows. No fire. The only light came from the torches in the hallway, shining through the bottom of the door. I reopened the door and left it cracked. It was enough to see the silhouettes of the furniture in the room. Arms outstretched, I crossed to Alon's desk.

Papers littered it, leaving hardly any space for the wood underneath to be seen. Anxiety rose inside me. I picked up the first paper I saw and held it toward the light from the door. It was full of writing thrown about the paper with no logical order. It wasn't the formal writing Adira told me to look out for. I placed it back down exactly where I had picked it up. My heart sank as I scanned the scattered papers. There was no way I could go through all of these without Alon noticing they had been moved.

Giving up on the desktop, I opened his top drawer where there were more papers, but they were blank. I closed it.

In the drawer below was a neat pile of papers with writing on them. I sorted through them. Lists, letters, all jumbled together. My pulse climbed. This was impossible.

Then I touched something different. Smooth parchment. The ink was darker and the script more elegant. It didn't belong. There were two pages of the same writing.

I folded them together and headed straight to the door to get more light. The door swung open before I reached it.

"Your Highness."

A small shot of relief loosened the knot in my chest as Richard stood in front of me and not Alon. I moved the papers behind my back.

"Is everything okay?" he asked, arching his brow.

"Of course. I was looking for Alon," I said, knowing I could easily mislead him about what I was really doing. "I had a couple questions for him about my trip to Nefali. I'm getting so very excited." I plastered on my signature princess smile.

"Oh. Well, may I answer any of them for you?" His eyes stayed fixed on my face as if he was searching for something.

"No, that's okay. I'll come back later when Alon is around," I answered, taking a sidestep to get around him. Paper crinkling surfaced from my back.

Richard's eyes zeroed in on where the noise came from.

"I think I will wait in my room until then," I said, moving away from him.

"Your Highness, what do you have behind your back?"

Heat traveled up my body. "It's...it's nothing. A piece of paper with my questions for Alon." I waved one of the papers in the air trying to feign indifference.

"May I see it?" Richard asked, extending a hand toward me.

"You know what, my questions are quite silly. I think I'm a little nervous about going to a different kingdom." I offered him a tense smile, and placed the paper behind my back again.

He didn't return the smile. His expression didn't change as he kept his hand out for the paper. "I don't want to ask again."

I'd never been afraid of Richard before, even if he was over the top and pushy at times, but there was something different in the sound of his voice and the way his bloodshot eyes stared me down.

I withdrew my hand from behind my back and placed a paper in his while sliding the other in my pocket. I pressed my lips together, feeling the heat crawl up my neck as he read it.

He released his breath. "Have you read this?" he asked with a tone I knew very well. It was the same one my father used with me when he was disappointed.

"Have you?" he asked, raising his voice.

"No, I haven't. I promise. I don't even know what it is."

His eyes flicked to the paper in his hand and back to me. For a moment they were saddened, highlighting the dark circles underneath them. But that look didn't last. "Come with me," he said. His fingers clamped around my arm.

"Wait. Richard, what are you doing?"

He didn't answer.

He pulled me further down the hallway, and I stumbled deeper into the mountain. The relief I'd felt a heartbeat ago soured into something sickening.

"Where are we going?" I asked, my chest tightening with each step as the air around me felt thinner. I had never been this far before.

He didn't answer me, but I could see his lips moving like he was muttering to himself. I tried to pull my arm away from him, but his grip tightened.

"Where are you taking me?" My voice rose in pitch as fear took hold.

He cast me a glance before snapping his attention forward again. "This is the only way," he said under his breath.

Richard quickened his steps as the light around us faded. No more torches lit the way, but he didn't stop. He continued to pull me forward, causing me to stumble over my feet a few times. Thankfully, it wasn't too long before a light could be seen ahead. Richard stopped in front of a door. He opened it and grabbed a nearby torch before ushering me in.

The room was small with a little cot pushed against the far wall and some crates scattered around.

"Richard." I faced him.

His eyes met mine and for a second, something flickered. Regret? Doubt?

"Please don't," I whispered

His lips curved downward as he placed the torch in a holder on the wall. "I'm sorry."

I ran forward, but the door shut. The latch locked. I pounded against the thick wood. "Don't do this! Please! Don't lock me in here."

"I'm truly sorry," Richard said, his voice muffled through the door. "But I must ensure you get to Nefali. I can't have you running away this time."

"I'll go! Please don't leave me here!"

The sound of footsteps growing faint was my only response.

I slumped against the door, forehead pressed to the wood. Trapped. The word pulsed in my mind until it was all I could hear. How could I have been so careless? How could Richard do this to me? I curled my hand into a fist and slammed it against the wood. Something shifted in my pocket, a faint metallic jingle. Hope bloomed in my chest. I reached into my pocket and pulled out the two tools, hands trembling but my hope rising. My breath caught. There was no keyhole. Whatever lock they had on this door couldn't be accessed from the inside.

Returning the tools to my pocket, I crumbled to the floor using the door as support. My chest compressed like the walls were closing in, and the air felt like it was thinning by the second. I dropped my head between my legs, trying to focus on my breath and failed—again.

"It will be okay. I will be okay," I whispered. Someone would wonder where I went and knock some sense into Richard. The plan was for Adira to meet up with me after the gathering. She would definitely wonder what had happened when I wasn't in my room. I wouldn't be here for long, so I needed to distract myself until someone came to let me out.

Lifting my head, I took another scan of the room, but my first observation had been accurate. There was nothing here besides a cot, a few crates, and a bucket.

It wasn't meant to entertain. It was a room to hold someone. A prison cell. My breaths quickened again along with my heart rate. This was too familiar. Too much like that cell in the palace.

I wasn't that girl anymore. I'd come too far.

I stood and shook my arms as if I could shake away those memories. I paced, telling myself over and over again someone would come. Richard would eventually come to his senses and realize he overacted. Whatever was in that letter—

I stopped.

I reached into my pocket and felt the piece of paper I had smuggled out. I tried to make sense of the writing. It was difficult to make out because every letter ran into the next one, and they included big loops. However, at the bottom was a signature. I jumped up a few lines and stopped when I recognized my name.

I slowly mouthed each word.

Preparations will begin as we anxiously await the arrival of Princess Talia, granddaughter of the late King Stephen and Queen Aleese. The union of our two kingdoms will bring everlasting strength and security. The people of Nefali will rejoice in their new queen.

CHAPTER 12

Raph

THE PLATFORM CREAKED BENEATH my boots as I shifted. Alon stood in front of me, addressing a sea of warriors gathered in the training field. He had asked me to join him for the announcement of the mission to Llycia, but besides that, nothing Alon was saying was new information. It was the same speech he gave at every gathering; however, the air buzzed with something different—anticipation.

I rubbed my thumb against the pommel of my sword, forcing myself to look at the crowd instead of him. The sun dipped low, staining the sky gold, but I could not shake the weight in my gut. Two hours had passed since I left Talia in her room, and the twist inside me hadn't eased.

"For nearly thirty years, we've waited for Landore to rise again." Alon's voice boomed over the crowd. "Not under the hand of a tyrant, but under its rightful heir. Under a leader who will unite Landore and bring it back to its former glory."

Cheers broke out around me. Cries of "Landore!" echoed like thunder. But to me, it didn't sound like victory. It sounded like a storm barreling toward something we weren't ready for.

Adira and Eitan stood near the front of the crowd, silent and observant. They should've been celebrating like everyone else. We should've been. This was the dream we had chased since childhood. The dream I owed him everything for. So why did the words taste hollow?

Adira gave me a quick glance out of the corner of her eye, and I saw the same unease I felt. Nothing was simple anymore. Not war. Not loyalty. And definitely not the truth.

Alon raised his hands, urging silence. "My fellow warriors..." He cleared his throat before pressing on. "Today, our wait ends. Today, we take back Landore!"

The crowd roared. Alon worked on quieting them again. His stiff gestures showed how uncomfortable he was. Richard was the one who usually handled the charismatic part of speeches, but he was nowhere to be seen.

Finally, Alon gained enough control to speak over the scattered voices. "With the support of the Kingdom of Nefali and the strength of our rightful heir, we will defeat Madden and save Landore."

"Lan-dore," someone shouted.

"Lan-dore! Lan-dore!" The chant rose.

Alon stepped back, signaling he was finished. The chant carried on. Some of the younger students jumped up and down in the front row, eyes alight with fire they didn't understand. Too young to be going to war, too young to know what it costs. A cluster of warriors at the back caught my eye. They stood with their arms crossed tightly across their chests, faces unreadable. Each bore a strip of white cloth wrapped around their forearm. There were dozens of them. Standing silent and still.

A chill raced down my spine. I didn't know what the cloth meant, but I knew it felt like resistance.

A figure leapt onto the platform.

Richard.

He moved fast, his face pale. He bent to mutter something in Alon's ear. Alon's entire body stiffened. His brows snapped together. My heart pounded louder than the chants. Something was wrong.

Eitan met my eye for a beat, and I jerked my chin toward Skyhall. He tapped Adira's arm, and they slipped through the crowd. I tracked them until they vanished into the trees. I wanted to jump out of my skin.

Alon raised his hand, turned, and stalked off the platform. I followed close behind while the chant continued around us. On the ground, Alon spoke to Richard who shook his head, but his eyes remained widened with worry as they darted toward Skyhall.

I edged closer, turning my head to hear better.

Captain Dareon stepped in front of me. "Raph, I would like to go over the list of those joining you in Llycia."

I peered around him. Alon and Richard were walking away. I locked my hands into fists.

"Some changes need to be made," Dareon pressed, moving into my line of sight again.

"Do whatever you see fit." I dipped my head and slipped behind the platform.

Adrenaline coursed through me as I rushed around the outside of the mass of warriors. I heard my name being called out a couple of times, but I didn't try to register who it was. Once under the coverage of the trees, I sprinted.

Something had happened to Talia. I could feel it in my bones.

I pushed harder up the mountain path. By the time Skyhall was in front of me, my heart was a drumbeat in my throat. I didn't slow down until I reached Talia's door. Without knocking, I burst through it.

Adira and Eitan were in the middle of her room. Talia's guard was unconscious against the wall. But Talia was nowhere in sight.

"Where is she?" I dropped to one knee and checked under the bed.

"Raph, breathe. We'll find her," Adira said, but her voice was tense.

"She might still be in Alon's study or maybe with her mother..." Eitan gave a quick look to Adira.

"I'll check with Mrs. Caffrey," Adira said, heading for the door.

"Kitchen," I said to Eitan.

He nodded and disappeared.

I bolted down the hallway toward Alon's study. The door was ajar. A lump formed in my throat. It's Skyhall. How much trouble could she have gotten in? Pushing the door fully open, I stepped in. It was dark, and empty.

I returned to the hallway ready to look outside of Skyhall. But a thought made me stop.

What if Talia was caught? I pressed my lips together, trying to think of what someone might have done with her. I whipped my head in the opposite direction that led deeper into the mountain.

They wouldn't.

I padded down the hall. I passed the other studies and storage rooms. The corridor narrowed and dimmed. I grabbed a torch off the wall and kept moving. I hadn't been this deep in the mountain since I was a boy and my curiosity got the best of me. Most people didn't know there was anything this far.

Light flickered ahead.

My stomach dropped, and I sped up. The air was cold and stale. When I reached the heavy wooden door emitting light, I grabbed the lock bar and yanked. But it didn't move. I pulled at it again, but nothing happened besides the sound of the bar hitting the door.

"Hello?" Talia's small voice called out.

"Princess." Relief and fury collided in my chest. "Are you okay?"

"Oh, Raph." Her exhale cracked with relief. "Please get me out of here." She was closer.

"I'm trying," I said, holding the torch closer to where the bar should slide out. "It looks like I need a key." I lifted the mechanism, frustration building. "Adira," I muttered.

"What's wrong?" she asked, fear creeping back into her voice.

"I'm not able to pick the lock."

"Why not?"

"It's one of Adira's designs."

"Then get her," she said.

"The lock was designed to be unpickable. The only way is with the key," I said, reexamining the keyhole.

"Raph, I can't stay here."

"I'll get you out." I placed my fist against the door. "Who did this to you?"

"It was Richard. He caught me leaving Alon's study. I would have fought back or at least tried to, but I never imagined he'd lock me up like a prisoner."

"This isn't right," I mumbled under my breath. "Did he say anything?" I asked.

"Just that he was sorry and there was no other way."

I gritted my teeth.

"But I found a letter from the king and queen of Nefali…"

"Did you read it?" I asked.

Her pause made my blood pump hot.

"I was able to hide one piece of the letter from Richard. I still have it."

"What does it say?"

"That they—they plan to marry me off to the prince of Nefali."

A dull roar filled my ears.

"Raph, did you hear me?"

I swallowed. "What?"

"This whole time they have been planning to marry me off to some prince to create a union between the two kingdoms." The anger in her voice switched to pain.

"No. That can't be true. Alon—they wouldn't—"

Her words snapped like a whip. "They have."

Something inside of me tore wide open. And in that moment, a thought I had wrestled with clawed back into my mind: staying loyal to Alon would mean losing her. "You won't be forced into anything," I said, moving closer to the door. "I won't let this happen. I promise."

"What do we do?" Her voice was almost a whisper.

"I'll get you out. Just hold on a little longer."

"Please hurry."

"I will."

It felt like betrayal to leave her locked away like a criminal. But if I acted without a plan, I'd be handing her right back to them, and I wasn't going to let that happen. Not this time.

CHAPTER 13

Jules

THE ROOM SMELLED OF iron and cold stone. Light emitted from a single torch attached to the wall, weak and uneven. There was nothing in the space that promised kindness. A simple table, a wooden stool, and a rack of tools were what accompanied me as I stood with my wrists chained, waiting.

The door scraped open behind me, but I didn't turn around. I knew why I'd been brought to the small room and who was coming.

Kasper's boots struck the floor in steady rhythm as he passed without a glance. He stopped at the table, bracing both palms against its edge. His shoulders were tight, like they carried more weight than the rest of him could stand.

The sight pulled me back to our first encounter. The two of us. The table. My wrists bound. My kidnapping. How foolish I had been thinking I could've escaped on my own. How invincible I'd believed myself to be.

The chains rattled against my wrists, but he didn't move.

Two days had passed since I'd last seen him, since he'd stormed into Gil's cell and left him broken. My skin crawled at the memory of each blow, each sound, while I stood helpless. Gil had been dragged out of his cell twice since then. It was my turn.

Kasper pushed off the table, picked up a length of metal from the rack, and set it down again with a clink. At last, he turned. His eyes found mine, shadowed and restless.

"Where is their camp?" he asked.

"I don't know." My voice sounded dull, even to my own ears.

His jaw flexed. He lifted the piece of metal again, rolled it in his palm, then slammed it on the table. "You do know. Tell me."

"I don't know," I repeated, eyes on a shadow trembling against the stone.

"You're one of them."

"I'm from Gasmere. I've never been to their base."

His boots scraped as he came closer, highlighting the dark crescents under his eyes. "Tell me how you got

Princess Talia and that rebel out of the palace. We know you were here that night."

"They were told of a hidden entrance into the palace." The words left me, but they didn't feel like my own. "They used powder to blast the wall open."

Silence. I glanced up.

His face flickered with surprise and his voice dropped lower, suspicious. "You gave me the truth. Why?"

"Because it doesn't matter." My wrists sagged against the chains, metal biting skin. "It doesn't change anything."

"Who told them about the passageway?" he asked.

"Some contact. They never said who."

The words fell flat, lifeless. Kasper studied my face for something, maybe fear, but I had nothing left to give.

"Who?" he pressed. "Was it a soldier? A servant?"

"I don't know."

He moved in closer, voice tight. "I want a name."

"I told you, I don't know."

His breathing quickened. "Yes, you do." He closed the distance with one step and lifted his hand. "You have to."

I flinched, eyes squeezing shut, waiting for the sting.

It never came.

I opened my eyes, his hand trembled. He let it fall uselessly to his side and turned away. He dragged the stool across the floor, the sound harsh and scraping, and sank onto it. His elbows found his knees, and his head sank into his hands.

I blinked. This wasn't the reaction I expected. But then again, nothing about my life made sense anymore. None of this was supposed to happen. The future I'd imagined was gone.

His fingers laced tighter into his hair, and he stayed bent over, silent. I should have cared what it meant, but the hollow inside me swallowed the thought whole.

The torch sputtered.

Kasper didn't move. Seconds stretched into minutes, until I lost count. The only sound was his breathing, ragged but controlled, as if he was fighting something I couldn't see. I stood there chained, waiting for the blow, the question, anything. Nothing came.

At last he lifted his head, eyes flat. Without a word he rose, the stool scraped back. He took hold of my chains and unhooked them from the wall. The weight of them pulled at my wrists as he guided me toward the door. We walked in silence. His grip was firm but distant. Without a pause or a look, he unlocked a cell and shoved me inside. The clang of iron rattled my bones.

I stumbled, caught myself, and only then realized the shape slumped against the wall.

Gil.

The torchlight cut across his face, swollen and darkened with bruises. His shirt was torn, dried blood streaking his chest. He lifted his head, and his lopsided grin tried to hold, though it faltered with pain.

"Hey, there." His voice was raw.

I froze. For two days I had allowed myself to drown in my own misery. I was in a trance, convinced there was no way out. But when I looked at Gil, I felt it. That sharp, gutting guilt.

"Gil..." His name cracked out of me as I stepped closer. "You look—"

"Like I fought a bear and lost?" He coughed, winced, but the corner of his mouth twitched. "You should see the other guy."

Tears pricked hot at the corners of my eyes. I wiped them away, ashamed. "I'm so sorry." I crouched in front of him. "I've been consumed in my own misery, thinking this was the end."

"Don't be sorry." His tone was soft but steady. "This isn't your fault. But you can't give up." He tilted his head toward me, eyes glassy but holding. "You never know what the future holds. I'm not willing to accept this as the end. I have a lot more life I want to live." He tried to laugh, but it broke into a grimace.

The cell closed in around me. His words hung in the cold air. I didn't answer, I couldn't. But somewhere deep inside, beneath the guilt and despair, something small flickered.

CHAPTER 14

Kasper

I FORCED THE SERVANT'S screams out of my mind as the prison door shut behind me. The dungeons were the only place I could escape the courtiers' clawing voices and my father's watchful eye. Down here, no one schemed for favor or tried to twist my words. But peace never lasted. The stone walls still carried the echoes of those I had broken.

"Put him with the others," I ordered Oliver, who stood stiffly by the door.

"Yes, Your Highness." He tipped his head, then nodded down the corridor. "And the rebels?"

"I'll deal with them tomorrow," I muttered, digging into the knot in my shoulder. I hadn't questioned either of them since Jules. Her lifeless stare still burned into my mind. Prisoners had never gotten to me before. I needed to shake whatever it was about her that kept getting under my skin.

"Very good, Your Highness."

I glanced down the hall to ensure we were alone. "Any update about what I asked you to look into?"

"Nothing unusual. No schedule changes or relocations to new areas of the palace," Oliver said. His fingers twitched at his belt. "Is there something more specific you'd like me to seek out, Your Highness?"

"No," I answered. The knot in my stomach twisted tighter. "Keep me informed if you hear anything."

"Of course, Your Highness."

When he was gone, I slipped into the small office tucked away by the cells. My key scraped in the lock and I shut the door behind me. The single candle on the desk barely lit the room, but it was enough. I logged the servant boy's name into the ledger, another meaningless line among dozens. None of them had yielded anything substantial but fear. I needed to try something else.

I pushed the ledger aside and reached under the desk, sliding out the folded sheet I kept hidden. My list. The map of every wing, hall, and hidden room I had searched. I traced a line where I planned to check next. My evenings belonged to these searches. Sleep had long stopped being an option. She was somewhere inside these palace walls, somewhere just out of my reach. But I would find her, because I had learned never to trust my father's word.

I shoved the list back into its place and stepped into the corridor, heading to my quarters to wash the blood off my hands.

"Long day, Your Highness?"

Sal's voice cut through the hall the moment I emerged from the stairwell. He sauntered toward me, coat half-buttoned, his gait unsteady. Even from where I stood I could smell the whisky.

"You missed a fine evening," he slurred. "A celebration of the progress that has been made."

"Progress?" I kept walking. He tried to keep pace.

Sal smirked with glassy eyes. "Three nobles already named. Turncoats, all of them. And tonight," he leaned closer, "I may have caught a whiff of a fourth."

"Accusations aren't evidence," I said, flatly.

"At least I'm producing something," he shot back, stumbling a step to keep pace. "The king praises me while you waste nights dragging stable boys and kitchen girls into cells only to release them. What have you shown him? Nothing. No rebels. No camp. No results."

I stopped and ground my teeth together hard enough to hurt. One more word and I'd—

"You've disappointed him. He wants rebel blood—"

"I'm quite aware of the king's desires."

Sal leaned closer like he couldn't help himself. "One might assume a prince with something to lose—someone, perhaps—would show a bit more urgency..."

I grabbed the front of his tunic and slammed him against the wall. His head hit with a dull thud.

"Don't," I growled, my breath hot against his face, "test me."

Sal's smirk faltered. His eyes flickered with fear beneath the whisky haze. I shoved him back against the wall one last time.

"Go sleep it off," I said coldly before walking down the corridor.

I moved through the palace without direction, caught somewhere between fury and exhaustion. Each step carried the echo of Sal's words. He was right. For all the blood on my hands, for all the sleepless nights, I had nothing to show. No spies uncovered. No rebel camp. No Lliana.

I rounded a corner too fast and clipped a wall sconce with my shoulder. It rattled. My eyes flicked to the end of the hallway, narrowing where I thought I saw movement. Two guards stood outside the familiar door of Princess Talia's old room. Although now it was her father who was locked away in there.

"Open it," I ordered, desperate to gain some useful information.

The guards scrambled, fumbling with the latch until the door creaked inward.

I stepped into the dim room. Light flickered from a hearth near the far wall. I stood with my arms hanging heavy by my sides and my throat tight.

"You couldn't sleep either?" A voice rasped from the far side of the room.

I dropped my hand to the pommel of my sword.

John sat by the fireplace, his face worn but calm in the glow of the embers.

"Why aren't you asleep?" I asked.

He chuckled. "I was. Pain woke me." He gestured to his bandaged foot. I'd overheard a report that the palace Healer believed the break had caused an infection in his bone. Pain was something he would always live with. "What about you, Your Highness? What drives you to a prisoner's room at this hour?"

I didn't have an answer. The crease between his eyebrows deepened.

"Sit," he said, nodding to the empty chair. "Unless you've come to kill me?" His voice was somber as if he expected that may be the reason but didn't fear it. I released my grip on the sword and stepped forward.

"Tell me what you know of the rebels. Where have they taken Talia? Where are they hiding?"

Silence stretched between us. Finally, his voice cut through, "Sometimes I think sleep avoids those who carry too much. The mind won't rest until the heart is heard."

I waited for more, but he stared into the fire.

"You speak nonsense. Answer me."

"Maybe." His voice was steady, almost gentle. "But I do know the look of someone who carries a burden too heavy."

"You know nothing about me." I bit down on my tongue, suppressing my rising frustration. Maybe I was too tired for this. I should have walked away. Yet I remained, rooted to the floor as if nailed there.

The fire cracked, shadows shifting across the walls.

"Your mother," John said softly, his gaze still on the flames, "what did she want for your life?"

His words speared straight through my chest. What was he playing at? Did he know I had no memories of her? Only fragments others had whispered. How she was full of life and love, the opposite of my father. "Enough! Tell me what you know about the rebels."

He released his breath, still watching the fire. "You already know I have nothing useful. That's not why you're here."

Heat crawled further up my neck. "Then why am I here?"

He finally looked at me, his gaze calm, unflinching. "Because you're battling with yourself. Torn in two. Between who you must be and who you wish you could be."

My nails dug into my palms. "You know nothing."

John shook his head once, sadness etched in the lines of his face. "You're in a hard place. But you're not without a choice.

I scoffed. "You're wrong."

He shrugged slightly. "Maybe. But what I see is a young heart trying to survive in a world that's never been kind to it."

Every word scraped against something raw inside me. He carried this calm, steady presence that pressed in like warmth I didn't want but couldn't push away. For a heartbeat I was tempted to tell him everything, lay it all down. It terrified me more than anything my father had ever done to me.

My fists curled tighter. "You know nothing of the world I've grown up in." I turned for the door, desperate to escape before his words dug any deeper.

"For what it's worth," he said behind me, "it's never too late to change your future."

The knob was cold beneath my hand. I didn't look back. I couldn't.

CHAPTER 15

Talia

SOMETHING SCRAPED IN THE dark. I jolted upright, breath ragged. No light. No sound. Just damp and cold and the ache in my body. The memory of Richard locking me away, the letter, and the fear taking hold when Raph didn't come back slammed into me. I curled tighter, tucking my knees to my chest. The wall beside the bed was wet, and my back stuck to it.

It could've been hours. A day. Several days. Time was broken. The letter crinkled in my pocket when I shifted, like it was mocking me. I squeezed my eyes shut and let the pressure rise. My hands fisted in the thin blanket.

"When will this all end?" The words burst out in a raw whisper. Every time I started to take control of my life something came along and knocked me straight on my back, taking my power away from me. My throat burned.

Metal scraped and I froze.

My cell door swung open and torchlight spilled across the floor, blinding me after too much darkness. I raised a hand to block it as I sat up.

"Princess," a voice said softly.

I blinked against the light. "Raph?" Three silhouettes stood in the doorway: Raph, Adira, and Eitan. Relief hit like a wave, knocking my breath loose. "You came," I murmured.

Raph stepped in, his expression pinched with concern, matching Eitan and Adira's. "Are you okay?"

I stood. "If you don't count how I spent the past who knows how lon—"

"Thirty-six hours," Eitan interjected.

I acknowledged his answer with a tilt of my head. "Thirty-six hours locked in a dark cell deep within a mountain. Oh, and learning the people I'm supposed to trust lied to me and plan to force me to marry someone I've never met. Sure, I'm okay."

They stared.

Raph moved forward, and for a second, I thought he might pull me into a hug, but he stopped short. "I came as soon as I could," he said quietly.

I wrapped my arms around my waist. "Thirty-six hours." My voice broke.

He flinched. "I tried…"

"We had to steal the key from my father," Adira said, clutching something in her hand. Her gaze lowered. "I'm sorry for what he did."

"It wasn't your fault," I said, pushing my frustration down.

"I can't believe he would do something like this." She gazed around the small room, and her eyes saddened.

A moment passed. "Can we please get out of here?" I asked, squeezing myself tighter. I didn't think the chill would ever leave my bones.

"Yes," the three of them said in unison.

We walked through the narrow hallway, and I expected to feel some sense of relief, but the weight hadn't lifted.

"They're in a meeting," Eitan said over his shoulder. The flickering torchlight in his hand cast shadows across the stone walls. "All of them."

"Do they know I'm free?"

Raph shook his head. "Not yet."

"Well, what are we waiting for?" I asked. "Let's storm in and demand the truth!"

The corner of Raph's mouth lifted.

"Raph said that's what you'd want to do," Eitan said with a smile. "But are you sure you want to confront them now?"

"Yes." My jaw clenched. "I agreed to be their symbol of hope and go to Nefali for them, but I didn't agree to lies and secrecy. I need to know everything, and catching them off guard might be our best shot."

Eitan dipped his head in agreement. I peered behind me to catch Adira's thoughts, but her gaze was fixed on the ground in front of her. Her eyebrows pulled tight.

The hallway widened and more light illuminated our path. I recognized the roughly carved doorway ahead. No one said anything as we stopped in front of them. Eitan and Raph stood on either side of me, but Adira stood back.

"You don't have to come," I said to her.

Her gaze lifted, eyes shining with unshed tears. She shook her head. "I need to hear what he has to say."

I grimaced.

"Talia," she half-stepped toward me, "this isn't him. Something has changed."

I closed the space between us and placed my hand on her shoulder. "Someone once told me fear can change even the best of us. But that still doesn't give him the right to lock me up."

"You're right."

I squeezed her arm, then stepped back to face the large doors. The muffled hum of voices leaked through the cracks. Raph glanced over at me.

I tried to swallow, but there was no moisture in my mouth. I placed my palms on the wood where the doors met, grounding myself with one steady breath. Raph and Eitan each took a doorknob. I nodded once.

The doors slammed against the stone walls when I strode into the chamber.

Conversations halted. Chairs scraped. Every pair of eyes turned to me, but I looked only for one.

"Your Highness." Richard shot from his seat, his hand disappearing inside his jacket. When it reemerged empty, his gaze darted to Adira. She stood to the left of me, twirling a small object between her fingers. The key. "Wha...what—"

Alon rose calmly. "What may we help you with?" he asked, voice steady, controlled.

My boots echoed as I stepped farther into the room, Raph, Eitan, and Adira flanking me like sentries. "You locked me in a cell like a traitor," I seethed.

Gasps rippled across the table, but no one interrupted.

"Because I uncovered your secrets."

Richard's face twitched, but Alon remained a statue.

"You plotted to marry me to a foreign prince without my knowledge. You wrote letters to Nefali using my name to make promises I never agreed to. And you used my future like it was a bargaining chip."

"What happened to you, Your Highness, should never have occurred," Alon said, flicking his eyes to Richard. "It was a rash decision, acted on without approval. We are sorry."

I blinked, caught off guard. "But not sorry enough to release me or tell me your plans for *my* life?"

Alon didn't respond, but he also didn't break his eye contact.

Richard spoke up. "We were never going to force you to marry the prince," he said with a strained laugh as he looked out among the other leaders. "The marriage arrangement was...an option. A strategic path. You were always going to have the final say."

"Why hide it from me?" I shot back. "Why keep it buried in letters and whispered meetings?" My gaze flicked to Nadav and Hafsa, who sat with tight expressions. I didn't have time to think of their betrayal and the pain it caused me.

"Because, Your Highness," Richard said as he released his breath, "you've made rash decisions in the past when you let your emotions drive you. We feared you'd sabotage something vital before understanding the weight of it."

I laughed, sharp and bitter. "So you decided for me?" I clenched my fists, hiding how my hands shook. "You call King Madden a tyrant, but you've made me a tool for your own ends. You're no better than him."

Murmurs stirred among the leaders.

"You say you fight for Landore's freedom." I raised my voice, "But how can you fight for it while silencing its people?" I took my time looking at every person seated around the table. They had to be aware something was going on in Aydencia. Some lowered their eyes. Others stared straight back.

"Freedom comes at a cost, Your Highness," Richard said.

I inhaled. "So you'll pass over the signs of unrest, dismiss the white cloths, downplay how my ship was sabotaged, and ignore that your people don't want a war?"

"She's right," came a voice at the far end of the table.

All eyes turned to a younger man who stood slowly, his shoulders squared. It was the same man I saw whispering to Richard in the hall.

"We've stopped listening. If we're not protecting our people's voices, then what are we fighting for?"

I locked eyes with him and saw it. Not just courage, but doubt and uncertainty.

Another voice rose up, louder and firmer. "There will always be unrest. That's the nature of war."

Many around nodded their heads in agreement. The younger man sat back down.

Alon stood there, eyes focused on me. "Although this *unrest* you speak of is unwanted, it isn't something to fear." His focus switched back to those around the table. "We can't let whispers of doubt dictate our course. Doubt will always be there no matter what path we choose." He looked at me. "You have every right to be angry. We should've told you from the beginning. But fear clouds judgment, yours and ours."

He paused. "You've always followed your heart. And while that's admirable, it can also be dangerous. You've witnessed what happens when emotions lead..." My chest tightened. "We won't force your hand in marriage. The proposal remains just that, a proposal. But we still need you to lead. We believe an alliance with Nefali is our best chance at winning this war." He pushed back his chair and stepped toward me. "Go to them as our representative, not our sacrifice."

I hesitated. "You expect me to trust you now?"

"No." His features softened. "Raph will go with you to ensure your safety and to ensure no one forces your hand again. Not them. Not us."

I peered over my shoulder. Raph stood tall with his gaze fixed on me. He didn't move or give me any sign of what to do or how he felt. It was my decision.

"I won't pretend we haven't failed you," Alon said, coaxing my attention back to him. "But I believe you still want to do your part for Landore and its people. We need you."

I exhaled. "I'll go. But I want a letter written to the King and Queen of Nefali informing them no marriage arrangement is on the table, straight away."

Alon's expression tightened, and Richard's mouth gaped.

"We will inform them of your choice," Alon answered.

Richard slammed his hands against the table and stood. "Excellent. We'll begin your departure at once." He turned to another leader and rambled off some instructions. I focused on Alon, who still stood away from the table staring at me. I didn't trust him, and I didn't know if I ever would again.

I tipped my head in his direction and then backed out of the room as the voices around the table grew louder. I would go to Nefali, not for them, but for all of Landore, for my father, Jules, and for Gil. Beneath the weight of that decision, a small, stubborn part of me clung to something I wouldn't let them touch: the quiet certainty that my future was no longer anyone's to decide.

CHAPTER 16

Jules

BANG. BANG. THUD.

"Jules," Gil hissed through the wall. His voice was hoarse, raw.

My boots slammed into the cell door. I ignored him and kicked again. Harder. The echo cracked down the stone corridor.

"What are you doing?" Gil's voice rose above the noise.

"I'm trying..." My breath came fast. I stepped back, nails digging into my palms. "To get his attention."

"He won't come, and kicking the door won't stop him."

"Well, I need to try *something*!" I slammed my palm against the wood. His groans through the night still played in my head. "I'm not going to do nothing while he uses you as a punching bag." One final kick rattled the hinges before I walked to the wall connected to Gil's. It hadn't taken the guards long to realize we were put in the same cell.

"It won't last forever." He tried to sound optimistic, but the shake in his voice stole any power from his words.

I tensed. He was right. The interrogations wouldn't last forever because he wouldn't last for much longer. "Something has to change *now*." My heel scraped against the stone. "And we have no idea what's going on out there." I dropped to the floor, the ache in my legs nothing compared to the fire in my chest.

"I'm frustrated too, but we—" He started coughing. "We need to wait it out a little longer."

I stared at my fists. Time is what he didn't have. They gave me a small morsel of bread and water each day, but not Gil. "But what if—"

"They'll come."

"A rescue team might be on their way," I said. "But we'd be fools not to admit they might not be."

Gil remained silent.

"I won't rot in this cell knowing I didn't do everything I could to stop this." I picked up the empty tray that had my daily rations and threw it against the door with a clang. The sound filled the room, but nothing followed.

No footsteps. No keys. Yet, I stayed still, waiting, hoping, but nothing. I exhaled and dropped my head into my hands.

Somewhere beyond the wall, Gil shifted. It had been four days since Kasper beat him to unconsciousness, and he could still hardly move. It didn't help that Kasper dragged him out everyday for another round of interrogations. I admired Gil's loyalty and belief in his fellow Aydencian warriors, but I couldn't see a reason as to why they would risk themselves to save us when their focus was on protecting Talia. Plus, we didn't have time to wait. I—we needed to come up with a plan to distract Kasper.

Grinding metal ripped through the silence, and I snapped upright as the door creaked open. A small, red-headed woman stepped in, clutching a bucket. She froze when our eyes met. Pity filled her face. She hurried inside, leaving the door cracked just an inch behind her.

"I don't have much time," she whispered, eyes darting back to the hall.

I stumbled to my feet. "Who—what are you doing here?"

"Shh." She glanced over her shoulder again. "My name's Catherine. I used to be one of Princess Talia's maids."

I blinked. "Are you...here to get me out?" I whispered. "What about Gil? And John?"

"Please." She looked around the cell. "I don't have much time." She moved closer. Streaks ran down her face. Tear tracks, carved through layers of dirt.

"What happened?" I asked.

She shook her head sharply, like it hurt. "It wasn't me. He took..." Her voice broke. "He took her." She covered her mouth to muffle the sobs.

I stepped forward. "Who?" My pulse jumped. "Talia?"

"No," she said, clutching the bucket tighter. "The prince. He's been interrogating everyone: maids, kitchen hands, even the stable boys. And now they're disappearing. Like...like Malenee."

My chest cinched tight as the memories I'd tried to repress since being captured again surged to the surface. I was back in that wagon, trapped with the other young women. I swallowed. "Talia's other maid?" I asked, pushing the fear aside and recalling what Talia had told me about the two maids who became her friends and helped her escape.

Catherine nodded, her free hand brushing away the fresh tears.

"Why? What does he want?"

"He's trying to weed out traitors, anyone aligned with the rebels or who helped Princess Talia escape."

"How many have disappeared?" I asked.

"Fifteen that I know of."

I pressed my knuckles to my lips and stepped closer. "We need to shift his attention," I said in a low voice. "Get him and the king to look outside the palace. If we create enough noise, maybe they'll believe the greater threat is out there."

Catherine's eyebrows pulled in. "How do we do that?"

I froze. My mind was blank but buzzing. "I...I don't know. But there has to be a way."

Footsteps echoed beyond the door.

Catherine quickly swapped the bucket in the corner for the one she brought. "I'll try to come back," she whispered. Fear was in her eyes, but something like hope was there too.

"Wait," I called out in a harsh whisper as she was about to shut the door. "Talia's father, John, is he okay?

"He's alive."

My shoulders dropped as the door latched shut. He was alive.

But for how long?

I shuffled to the corner of the cell and lowered onto the ground. "Gil," I whispered. "Gil."

"Yeah?" His voice was weak.

"I had a visitor."

"Who?" The edge in his tone sharpened. "Are you—"

"I'm fine. It wasn't him. It was one of the maids who helped Talia." I swallowed. "She said Kasper's been interrogating everyone who works in the palace, trying to uncover hidden rebels. Some have started disappearing."

Silence.

"Gil, she was terrified and exhausted. We have to do something."

"But how?" His voice was low, hollow. "He won't stop, not until every rebel is destroyed, not until I give up the location of Aydencia."

I clawed at the mortar between the stones. My fingers scraped until grit stuck under my nails. "You're right, but we can't let it get to that. We need to draw his attention away from you and the palace."

"So, a diversion?"

"Yes." I stared at the door. "Which means, how do we get them to believe there's a bigger threat outside of the palace?"

He let out a slow breath. "We do have connections out there. And they've caused good distractions before."

"Gil, they're kids!"

"I know, I know. But they're our only contacts in Llycia, and they're resourceful."

I hesitated. "Even if they agreed to help, we'd have to get in contact with them first," I said, pressing my lips together. "Didn't Raph mention they had contacts inside the palace?"

"Yes, but how would *we* find them?"

"Right...How did Raph contact the Shades?"

Gil exhaled. "I don't know."

I tipped my head up at the ceiling as if the answer might be carved into the stone. For a second, I believed we had a plan that could work, that we could do something.

"Wait a minute..."

"What?" I asked, placing my palm on the stone wall.

"After Raph and I saved Scat from those poachers, he mentioned a yellow ribbon and said that's how he knew something was up. I thought it was a weird comment, but what if it's a code? Like a signal between them..."

"Okay..." I lowered my hand. "But we would still have to figure out what colors they use and what they mean."

"There might be one other person who knows how to contact them."

"Who?"

"Stella. She helped us with the disguises the night of the ball."

"Right," I said, vaguely remembering them mentioning they visited a friend of Raph's. "So if we tell Catherine how to find Stella, then Stella could help point her to the Shades."

A pause. "Jules..."

"I know, but at least it's something. The only other option I can think of is talking with *him*..."

"No." His voice was firm. "You can't."

"But you're the one who said he was cracking and we could try to turn him?"

"Yes, he may be cracking, but he is also dangerous and unpredictable. I don't want you near him."

"Gil—"

"Promise me." His voice was laced with desperation.

"Okay. I won't." I exhaled. "We'll wait and see if Catherine comes back and inform her about Stella." I hesitated. "I just hope it's enough to make a difference."

"All we can do is try," Gil said softly.

A silence settled between us.

Gil whispered, "I used to dream of this."

I frowned. "What?"

"The fight. The war. The cause." He gave a weak chuckle that ended in a cough. "My parents raised me for it. From the moment I was big enough to carry a sword, my future was written. My schooling, my training, even the books I read were about becoming the best warrior for the cause. I didn't know there was anything else to want."

I pressed my palms to the ground. "And now?"

He hesitated. "Now I wonder if the cost is too high."

The weight of his words sank deep.

"I thought dying for the cause would mean something," he continued. "That it would be noble or brave." His voice dropped. "But after seeing those villages...all that destruction." He swallowed. "Now I'm wondering if any of this is worth it."

My throat tightened. "I think I understand what you mean."

Gil was quiet for a long moment. "Do you ever wonder who we'd be if no one had told us who we were supposed to become?"

I gave a humorless laugh. "All the time."

He went quiet again.

"All I wanted was to make a difference," he said. "But if all of this: burned villages, innocent people getting hurt is the result..."

I leaned my head back against the stone. "Maybe the difference isn't in what has happened but in what we choose to do next."

CHAPTER 17

Raph

THE DOCKS SMELLED OF damp wood and salt, the air thick with the sharp, earthy tang that came before the rain. Clouds gathered over the harbor, restless and gray, seeming to reflect how I felt. I paced the worn planks as I scanned the bay. Sea birds cried out, sails flapped in the wind, and somewhere down the row of docks, sailors argued over cargo weight. Finally, the port master appeared in front of two storage crates. He yelled orders about the crates to the men standing nearby and then faced my direction. He squinted as I walked toward him.

"You the one heading out at dawn?" he called.

I nodded. "I want to put eyes on the ship, check over the supplies, and I need confirmation the passage is clear."

"That all?" he asked, not bothering to hide his annoyance.

"We can't be too careful. Not with what happened last time."

His lips pressed into a straight line. "Hold on." He riffled in his chest pocket, eventually pulling out a little black book. "A scouting ship was supposed to report back last night...nothing yet."

"Nothing?"

He closed the book. "Probably delayed by weather. It's the season."

The weather couldn't have been that bad. Adira and Eitan had left for Llycia that morning. "We can't sail unless we know it's clear," I said.

"Give them the day. They will probably report back by noon," he said, pocketing the book. "Let me grab the ship's manifest."

As he turned toward the supply shed, I caught sight of something white tied to the post. Then another, hanging from a rope ladder. Dozens hung scattered across the docks. A knot formed in my chest. None of this felt like something to be ignored. Not the missing scouting ship, not the way Alon had so easily offered I accompany Talia to Nefali. Something had changed his mind, but what? Nothing sat right. I didn't know what or who to trust anymore.

The port master returned with a scroll tucked under his arm.

"Cargo's all accounted for," he said, handing it to me. "We'll double-check the hull after midday. Wind's shifting. We might get a quick storm this afternoon."

"What about the rudder line?"

"It's been checked, like always, but you are free to go and take a look yourself. I have other matters to attend to." He headed back to the crates where the men were lifting the last one onto the knarve.

I unrolled the papers and read them line by line. A low hum filled the air, snagging my attention.

Voices.

Dozens of them.

I rolled the scroll back up and walked toward the edge of the dock to get a better view. Up the incline, where the road curved toward the shops, a crowd was forming. They were headed straight for the docks, arms raised, white cloths tied to staffs or flapping in their hands.

"Peace, not blood! Peace, not blood!" they chanted over and over again.

A banner rippled in the breeze: *War is not freedom!*

These were the voices Alon was ignoring.

The crowd stopped in front of the docks, blocking the path.

"Get them moved!" The port master yelled from behind me.

A handful of dockhands shouted at the crowd and waved their arms for them to move. But the protesters' voices grew louder.

I moved closer.

Their chanting broke. A line of Aydencian warriors made their way down the street. Other Aydencians had stepped out of the shops to witness everything, but they moved out of the way to let the warriors pass, except for one.

Somebody ran alongside them, weaving through the gaps, making their way to the front. Her blonde hair whipped behind her, undone from its usual braid.

Talia.

Her guard was chasing after her.

I shoved through the nearest pocket of protesters. "Out of my way," I shouted, slamming my shoulders into backs.

Several elbows jabbed my sides in response.

I broke through as the warriors reached the edge of the street. Talia skidded to a stop, panting, eyes flashing as she took in the sea of protesters. Her gaze passed over me and then flicked back.

"What are you doing here?" I asked, grabbing her arm to move her out of the way, but there wasn't enough time because the front line of protesters had dropped their chants and were moving back up the street, closing us in. I stepped forward and raised a hand toward them. But they ignored me as their voices raised in incoherent shouts. The warriors passed in front of Talia and me, led by Captain Dareon, who was ordering the protesters to disperse.

A younger man with a white cloth tied around his wrist extended his fist in the air. Dareon caught the man's wrist and shoved him backward, harder than necessary. He was only going to escalate the situation. The boy stumbled hard, his head nearly hitting the stones. Dareon didn't even look back.

The crowd surged forward.

"Force them back!" Dareon ordered.

A scream sliced through the air. The protesters buckled as warriors pushed them back. Cries multiplied. I opened my mouth, but it was too late to do anything.

I tightened my hold on Talia and yanked her in front of me. Pulling her against my chest, I lowered my mouth to her ear. "Stay close." Bodies pressed in around us. I briefly searched for Talia's guard but couldn't see him anywhere. Someone stumbled into me, so I shoved them off but quickly had to turn and shield Talia from a swinging elbow. She hadn't been paying any attention because her eyes had locked on something else.

"No!" she shouted and tore free from me.

A boy was curled in a ball as feet trampled over him. Talia ran toward him, hands outstretched. "Get back!" she cried, shoving as many bodies away from the boy as she could.

A voice rang out, ragged and furious. "This is your fault! You brought this on us!"

Talia froze, her eyes wide as if she had been struck.

"You never should've come," the voice snarled before disappearing back into the thrum.

Bodies rammed into her, but she didn't move.

"Talia!" I shook her shoulder. "The boy."

Her eyes widened.

I grabbed the boy's arm and lifted him. Talia tried to shield us as I held the boy in my arms. He was no older than twelve. She led, doing her best to make a path to the edge of the chaos.

We found a barrel and placed the boy down. Talia scanned over his body and started whispering in his ear. The boy's whole body convulsed as tears ran down his cheeks. A whistle shrieked through the noise, followed by the thunder of more boots. A new wave of warriors cut through the fray like a blade, led by Alon himself.

Something loud and bright like lightning filled the sky, which stunned everyone into silence.

Alon raised his voice. "Disperse. All of you. Go home."
No one moved.

His eyes scanned the crowd. "Leave now or be taken by force and tried for obstruction."

Murmurs broke out, followed by the sound of shuffling. The crowd slowly dissipated.

Alon stepped forward. His gaze swept over the mess and landed on us. He pointed in the direction of Sky-hall, obviously ordering us to meet him there. He relayed some commands to the warriors around him. Talia and I exchanged a look, then peered back at the boy, but he was no longer on the barrel. A woman held him in her arms and hugged him tightly to her chest. She proceeded to carry him up the street.

Talia took a step toward them, chest rising and falling. "I couldn't stop it," she said, her voice barely audible.

I grabbed her wrist. "He'll be okay."

Her lips grew thin, but she didn't pull away.

A glint of red trickled down her eyebrow. "You're hurt," I said, pulling her in front of me.

She lifted her hand toward her face. "Where?" She flinched when her finger pressed against her eyebrow.

"Come on, let's go get you cleaned up," I said, placing a hand on her back to guide her forward. The cut was small, but it split something open in me. I should've stood up to Alon, demanded he listen, and fought for her instead of trying to appease him. Maybe then none of this would've happened.

I wouldn't make that mistake again.

The crowd had thinned, but a lingering tension clung to the streets. Whispers and eyes followed us all the way to Skyhall. By the time we reached the front steps, the wind had picked up and rain threatened but hadn't yet fallen.

Inside, the halls were dim. Empty. Talia rubbed her arms, her shoulders tight. I kept my hand on her back, guiding her toward the men's wing.

She slowed, heels skidding slightly. "Where are we going?"

"To clean that cut," I said, applying light pressure to her back.

"I'm fine," she muttered, brushing her hair forward. "Besides, I thought Alon wanted to see us?"

"He can wait."

She hesitated, then nodded and followed me down the hall and up the narrow steps to my room.

"There's another level?" she muttered to herself.

At my door, I stepped aside and let her enter first. It wasn't much. Her eyes flicked over the cramped space. A small desk, a bed, and a washstand. Yet something about her gaze made my stomach twist.

I stepped in and kept the door open. "Sit," I said, nodding toward the end of the bed. I crossed to the basin and soaked a cloth.

Talia did as I asked and sat stiffly on the edge of the bed. Her eyes fixed on the floor and her hands folded tightly in her lap. I kneeled in front of her. "This might sting," I warned, then gently pressed the cloth to her brow.

She flinched and her lips parted slightly, but she didn't speak. Her face was inches from mine. I could see every emotion in her stormy and uncertain eyes. My hand dropped from her brow, hovering near her cheek. All I could think about was how soft her lips had felt against mine.

She shifted.

I pulled back, forcing my focus back to her cut.

"Why does it feel like everything's unraveling?" she whispered.

I didn't have an answer for her. Only questions that kept multiplying.

"They blame me." Her voice caught, barely above a breath. "They don't want this. They don't want me."

"This isn't your fault."

Her eyes glistened, fixed on the floor. "I thought I was doing what was best for everyone." Her lips trembled as she finally looked at me. "But what if I've been wrong?"

A soft knock echoed from the doorway. Talia jerked back. I turned to see her guard in the doorway, breathless.

"Alon wants to speak with you both in his study."

Talia rose quickly, avoiding both our eyes.

We followed him to Alon's study in silence.

I opened the door, and Talia stepped through.

Inside, Alon stood with his arms crossed in front of his desk. Nadav and Hafsa stood across from him, their expressions reserved.

"Close the door," Alon said once we entered.

He waited until we had joined the small circle.

"You're leaving for Nefali," Alon said. "At midnight."

Talia's shoulders went rigid. "What?"

Alon exhaled. "The unrest is spreading. Today confirmed it. You're no longer safe here."

"But we haven't—" Her voice cracked. "You haven't even sent word to the king and queen of Nefali. What if they—"

"We don't have time," Alon interrupted. "Nadav and Hafsa will help figure that out on the way."

"We'll explain the circumstances," Hafsa added gently. "Our royals will understand."

Talia narrowed her eyes and turned to me, missing the side glance Nadav gave Hafsa. Through her eyes, Talia begged me to say something.

I clenched my jaw. I wanted to argue. To fight this. To demand more time. But I could only see the cut on her brow. The boy in the street. The crowd. The chaos.

"You're not safe here. Not anymore," I said.

She looked away. "And I might not be safe in Nefali either."

"You have nothing to fear, Your Highness." Nadav said, placing his hand over his chest. "We'll protect you."

"I don't need your protection," she replied, but looked back at me.

I wanted to promise her I wouldn't let anything happen and that I wouldn't let her be forced into anything, but I was just as unsure as she was.

Alon broke in. "Nefali wants this alliance as much as we do. You'll be an honored guest, not a sacrifice. But to get you there safely and without stirring more unrest, you have to leave tonight—quietly."

I studied Alon, searching for any hidden sign about what his endgame might be in all this. There was a time when I would've followed him without question. But my blind trust in him was gone. In its place was a single vow: I would protect Talia, even if it meant turning my back on everything Alon had given me. A plan started to form in my mind.

Talia straightened her back, seeming ready to argue.

I leaned toward her. "It's safer for *everyone* this way," I whispered.

She softened and looked at Alon. "Okay."

"Good," he said with a nod. "Gather your things. You leave at midnight."

We backed away.

"Raph, stay." Alon raised a hand, halting me mid-step. "We need to go over a few things."

I opened my mouth and glanced at Talia. She gave me a tight smile and turned. I watched her go, every instinct screaming not to let her out of my sight. But I stayed rooted, needing all the information I could get if I was going to successfully protect her from what lay ahead.

CHAPTER 18

Talia

THE LIGHTS FROM THE city blurred in the distance, soft and flickering before fading from sight as the ship pressed toward the passageway out of Aydencia. Salt filled the air. I wrapped my arms tighter around myself as the night wind bit through my layers.

The sails snapped above me as the ship took its first sharp turn. Aydencia's jagged skyline disappeared behind the mountain. Raph stood at the helm, back stiff as he focused on maneuvering the ship safely. We hadn't taken a knarve. Alon ordered for us to take a smaller vessel, fewer hands required to sail it and its absence less likely to be noticed by the dockhands.

Hafsa and Nadav lingered near the sail lines waiting in case Raph called an order. It was only the four of us. Apparently, it was safer this way, along with leaving under the cover of night. I stepped beside Raph. His gaze stayed locked ahead.

"How can you see anything?" I asked, squinting into the darkness.

"Not really necessary. The mountains never move." He grunted as he turned the wheel. "You'd think a ship this small would be easier to handle, but the smallest gust sends it off course."

"Can I help?"

The ship lurched forward. Raph quickly jerked the wheel in the opposite direction. The tension on the rudder released, and his shoulders dropped a little. "Almost in the clear." He tipped his chin toward a narrow seam of stars ahead. An opening between the mountains. He steered the ship toward the strip, and the sliver grew wider. But my mind was still in Aydencia with the protest and the voices slicing through the crowd like a blade.

This is your fault.

"What do you think the people will say?" I whispered.

"About what?"

"When they find out I left for Nefali. That this war is one step closer to starting." My hands tightened around the rail in front of me.

Raph didn't answer right away. "That protest wasn't your fault. This isn't your fault."

"I still don't know if Nefali is the right choice," I admitted. "I don't know if they'll help us against King Madden or...use me..."

Raph's grip shifted on the wheel. He looked at me, and something hardened in his eyes. "I won't let that happen," he said.

I lowered my gaze as heat spread across my cheeks. I forced a breath, steadying the rush in my chest, before leaning my weight on the rail. "Do you think we can trust them?" I asked, watching Nadav and Hafsa.

He followed my gaze, eyes narrowing. "I don't know."

The silence between us stretched as I observed them talk with one another in hushed whispers. "Say I said no," I murmured. "To going to Nefali and being their spokesperson. Say we turned this ship around and headed to Llycia instead. Team up with Adira and Eitan and end this before an actual war starts." I held my breath.

He huffed, the ghost of a laugh. "I'd say it's not the worst plan I've heard. And I'd be lying if I said I hadn't thought of it already."

"Raph, I'm serious." I looked him in the eye. "I don't think Nefali is the right choice and neither is this war. We would be forcing this on the people of Landore without their consent. They might not want it." My resolve took root. "No. We need to finish this with as minimal bloodshed as possible."

"Whatever you decide, I'm with you." His gaze was unwavering. My mouth went dry, and suddenly the cloak I had wrapped around me felt too warm. He removed one hand from the wheel to face me. "I'm sorry." His apology was almost swallowed by the wind, but it hit me like lightning. "For what happened. For your father. For Jules. For Gil." He closed his eyes for a fraction.

"Raph, stop," I cut in. "You need to stop blaming yourself."

"Please." He stepped closer, his voice raw. "I need to say this." Heat rose at the base of my neck. "I'm sorry for keeping my distance. For blindly obeying Alon, thinking it would solve my problems. I was blind, choosing to ignore the signs in front of me." His voice thickened. "I stopped listening to my friends. To you. To my own heart." The space between us narrowed. His gaze flicked from my mouth back to my eyes, and the air seemed to hum.

Something inside me jolted in response. I'd hoped and dreamed for this moment to happen, for him to finally open up and let his guard down. To let me in.

"You're not the only one who has been blind." My words came soft, unsteady. "You were right. I buried pieces of myself to fit a shape others made for me. I thought it was the only way to save everyone. But maybe there's a way to make a difference without losing myself." My eyes stung with unshed tears.

"I'll follow you wherever you go, Princess." He waited for a beat, eyes full of fire and certainty I'd never seen before. "Just give me the orders."

I let his words hang between us, afraid they would disappear like a dream. I closed my eyes for one small instant, letting the answer leave my lips before I could stop it. "Llycia."

His answer came immediately and so did the space between us. "Done." He walked away from me, silently moving across the deck. I followed, not understanding what he was doing but with a sinking feeling in my gut. His hand drifted toward the dagger at his belt.

"Raph," I warned, barely above a whisper.

He didn't answer.

Hafsa had her back to him, helping Nadav secure a rope. Nadav looked up, seeming to sense something, but it was too late. In one swift movement, Raph grabbed Hafsa from behind, twisted her arm across her chest, and pressed his blade to her side. Nadav pivoted, one hand lifted in defense as the other moved to his belt. His fingers brushed the hilt of his sword, but he didn't draw it.

"Raph, what's going on?" Nadav asked.

Raph didn't speak, but he kept his eyes locked on him. I moved closer.

"How about we talk about this," Hafsa said. She hadn't attempted to fight back. She stayed poised, breathing steadily.

"Like you talked to Talia about the real reason she was going to Nefali? Your words don't mean much." Raph tightened his hold on Hafsa.

Nadav wrapped his hand around his pommel. Hafsa gave him a look, and Nadav released his hold.

"This isn't the way to handle this," Nadav said, raising his hands in surrender.

"Neither is handing her over to your king and queen to be forced into a marriage she doesn't want." His voice stayed low and clipped. "You should've told us the truth." There was pain in his voice. Maybe I wasn't the only one hurt by their betrayal.

"We were going to," Hafsa said calmly. "After we left Aydencia..." She looked at me. "We were going to tell you everything."

"When it was too late for me to say no?" I snapped.

"No. We were going to stand by you no matter what you decided." Hafsa's eyes held nothing but sincerity.

"Why wait?" Raph asked, not releasing her or the dagger.

Hafsa was quiet for a moment. "Because we didn't know who to trust or what might happen if we told you."

"We couldn't afford to break ties with Aydencia," Nadav spoke up. "Nefali needs this alliance just as much."

"What do you mean?" I asked.

Nadav and Hafsa shared a look and she dipped her head as if giving him permission.

"The king and queen of Nefali were always willing to help in the removal of King Madden," Nadav continued. "But their motives aren't purely altruistic. For them, their kingdom comes above all else, and the wealth of Nefali has declined over the past thirty years due to the closure of Landore's borders. Their goal is to get the borders open again to ensure the health of their kingdom."

"But the other kingdoms haven't closed their borders. Can't you trade with them?" I asked.

"It's not that simple. Landore used to act as a hub for the four kingdoms thanks to its location. Throughout the years our king and queen have tried to keep up trading relations with Tro'ish and Vasdere, but the distance has caused difficulties. Many ships have been claimed by pirates or the sea. Over time Tro'ish has cut themselves off completely. And Vasdere is not willing to take the risk anymore. They constantly live in fear King Madden will declare war with them since they are the smallest kingdom and since the late queen was a Vasderian."

I rubbed the back of my neck. "I had no idea all of this was going on."

"How could you?" Nadav said.

"So their plan was to force me to marry?" I asked, unable to hide the disgust in my voice.

"Yes," Hafsa cut in. "But you have to understand for our people marriage is an agreement between two families, one where the goal isn't to find love but to grow one's power or social standing."

"How awful." The words left my mouth before I realized.

"That's how I always saw it too." Hafsa gave me a playful smile and then winced. The tip of the dagger must have poked her.

My heart pounded. I didn't know what to believe, but I couldn't help but feel like this wasn't right. "Raph, let her go.".

He didn't move. "We still don't know if they're telling the truth. They could be saying anything to get you to Nefali."

"We meant what we said," Hafsa answered. "We were never going to force you to go if you didn't want to. That still stands."

I leveled Raph with a look. IIc held her for a moment longer. Then he exhaled through his nose and stepped back, lowering the blade.

Hafsa stepped away, calm as ever. "There's one more thing that might help you trust us," she said, moving next to Nadav. She didn't look at him. She focused on me. "My allegiance to Nefali runs deeper than anyone in Aydencia knows," she said slowly. "Not even Alon."

Raph tensed.

Hafsa hesitated and Nadav wrapped his arm around her waist. "I'm the daughter of Nefali's king and queen."

Her words knocked the air out of me.

"You're..." I stared at her. "A princess?"

She gave me a soft smile. "By birth, yes. Though I gave up my title a few years ago," she said, leaning into Nadav. He squeezed her waist.

I blinked, trying to sort through the questions flying across my mind. I looked at her, remembering how she always carried herself. So poised. "Gave it up?"

"Like I said, I wasn't a big fan of arranged marriages," she said with a wink.

"So your parents..." I started.

Raph spoke as I couldn't seem to finish my thought. "Why did they send you to Landore?" His eyes narrowed.

"We never lied about that," she said. "They might have disowned me as their daughter, but they couldn't deny my abil—" Nadav nudged her in the side. "Our abilities." She smiled at him.

Nadav added, "We were sent to gather intel about the state of Landore and King Madden."

"And when you reported back about Aydencia?" Raph asked.

"They were thrilled. They saw an opportunity for an alliance. An alliance they believed was necessary, especially if there was a living heir."

"So they could marry me off to their son. Your brother," I mumbled the last part.

"I didn't choose to be a princess," Hafsa said gently. "I was born into it. I know what it's like to be told who to become, what you're worth, and who you belong to."

A familiar ache twisted in my chest.

She stepped closer. "I would have stood beside you in Nefali. I swear it. Not as a spy. Not as a former princess. But as someone who knows what it means to have to fight for your voice."

I studied her for a long moment. Her hands were at her sides. Her breathing steady. I looked at Nadav. He didn't say anything, but his stance echoed Hafsa's, open. Raph's jaw flexed. A pause passed between us before the tension in his face relaxed.

"Then you'll help us get to Llycia?" I asked. "And help us to find Adira and Eitan and regroup, so we can figure out how to end this on our own terms?"

"Of course," Hafsa said.

"It would be an honor." Nadav dipped his head.

"We'll need to adjust course," Raph said, making his way to the helm.

"I'll help," Nadav called after him.

"That was quite the ambush." I overheard Nadav say to Raph before their words got lost in the wind.

I turned back toward the sea, gripping the railing. Hafsa lingered nearby.

"So you and Nadav?" I glanced over my shoulder where Nadav and Raph stood at the helm.

"We fell in love." Her focus shifted back to me. "But our choice of love over what our families wanted came with great sacrifice." Wisps of her hair blew across her face as she looked into the distance. "I, too, was in line for the throne."

"What happened?"

"It's a long story," she said with a mischievous grin, tucking her hair behind her ear.

"I think we have the time," I said with a grin of my own.

She laughed. Then froze and squinted into the distance. Dawn was a few hours out, but the moon was full. A shape emerged on the horizon.

It was still too dark for me to make out what it was. "What is it?"

"Nadav!" she yelled as she grabbed my wrist and pulled me with her toward the helm. "Starboard!" she called while we climbed the stairs.

Raph and Nadav looked in the same direction the shape had been.

"What is it?" I asked again.

Nadav's eyes squinted into the horizon. "A ship."

"Could be the scouting ship that hadn't returned yet," Raph muttered, though doubt edged his voice.

"It's headed straight toward us," Hafsa cut in. "And fast."

Raph raised the spyglass, peering through the lens. His shoulders tensed. "It's not one of ours."

CHAPTER 19

Kasper

MY HORSE'S HOOVES STRUCK the wet cobblestone, sharp and steady in the pattering rain. Each droplet stung my face like ice pellets. I rode through the palace gates and inhaled, trying to flush out the smoke clinging to my lungs. The fires had mostly held to the shops on King's Court, thanks to the rain. But three shops endured too much damage and would need to be rebuilt.

A stable boy raced up as I dismounted outside the stables. His eyes flicked to my soot-streaked cloak. I handed him the reins. "Walk him," I said, drawing his attention to my face. "Don't let him cool too fast."

"Yes, Your Highness." He bowed his head and led Strider into the stables.

I straightened. My back taut. Smoke itched behind my eyes. The sun had set hours ago. I had a few hours, maybe less, before the next transfer of prisoners I'd have to oversee. That was enough time to clean up and maybe get a few minutes of rest—which was more than I'd gotten in days.

The palace doors gave a hollow thud behind me, closing me in like a crypt. The corridor was empty for once, which was a welcoming sight. I exhaled. I didn't have the energy to deal with scurrying servants or courtiers looking to catch my ear. I rolled my neck, cracking out the tension. Turning a corner, I shook my head, flinging droplets from my soaked hair.

"Eww!"

Lady Celeste stood a few feet ahead, arms raised to shield her face. Behind her, three of Talia's former ladies-in-waiting bit their lips in an attempt to not be caught giggling.

"How dare—" Celeste's expression snapped into something more graceful as she spotted me. "Oh, Your Highness." Her bow was an endeavor at grace. But it looked more comical in its exaggeration. "I didn't recognize you." Her eyes flicked from the soot marring my face to my soggy appearance. "We missed your presence at your father's dinner."

I bit the inside of my cheek, knowing I'd be in trouble for missing another event. "I had other matters to attend to."

Her lashes fluttered. "Of course! I do not doubt that. Though I was desperately hoping to catch your ear for a moment tonight. If I may, I will walk with you," she said, already claiming my arm with a firm enough grip to declare it would be pointless to shake her off. A waft of rosewater and something sharp wrapped around me. She flicked her fingers. "Ladies."

They bowed swiftly and continued down the hall, heels clicking. I watched them pass. There had been more of them before. I was sure of it.

"I heard about the fires," she said, guiding me toward the less trafficked halls. "Is it true the dressmaker's shop was destroyed in that fire? Everyone is in such a panic."

"It'll get rebuilt."

"With everything going on, it's hard to believe we're even in Landore anymore. The rebels growing strong enough to infiltrate the palace. Not once but twice. And on your wedding night..." Her sigh felt more fitting for those hobbled stages they put up during festivals in the villages. "One can't help but wonder if all of this started the moment the 'lost princess' was found..."

I stopped walking. "What are you getting at, Lady Celeste?" We reached the end of the hall.

She faced me, lips pressed together. "Only that people are nervous. Not everyone is convinced the king's strategy is...working." She glanced over her shoulder at the dead hallway behind us, yet still lowered her voice. "There's talk. Whispers in the corridors. Some nobles are leaving. Even my father mentioned moving us to some village for a while." She scrunched her nose like she'd tasted something sour.

"My father says it's only a matter of time. That if things don't change..." Something in her eyes flickered. It almost looked like fear. "He says the court is unraveling." She looked at me. "You're the heir, Kasper. You need to do something."

What more could I do? I was already extinguishing fires, chasing rebels, interrogating servants, making pointless appearances at my father's parties. The light stung my eyes sharp enough to make me blink.

Celeste squeezed my arm. "If nothing changes, there won't be a court left." Her gaze locked on mine. "This could be your chance to seize power."

Before I could answer, the sound of brisk footsteps echoed down the corridor. Celeste and I both turned as Mistress Pennier appeared at the far end of the hall, her posture straight and her expression disapproving.

"Your Highness," she called, her tone carrying the authority of someone who'd corrected me more times than I could count as a boy.

Celeste's hand slipped from my arm.

"His Majesty requests your presence," Mistress Pennier said, stopping before us. Her gaze flicked to Celeste, sharp and scolding.

Celeste bowed. "I enjoyed our conversation, Your Highness." She turned and walked away. Whatever she and her father were planning would have to wait. They only wanted my involvement if it served their own ambition, and I didn't have the time or energy to care.

When I looked back, Mistress Pennier was studying me with that pinched expression I'd long since learned meant concern. Her lips parted as if to speak.

"Not tonight," I said, turning away. I wasn't ready for her reprimands or reminders to rest.

I started down the corridor to the throne room.

Behind me, her voice followed, softer this time. "He's waiting in the war room."

My steps faltered, chest tightening as I changed course toward the east wing, toward the war room. I'd never stepped foot inside. Not once. I'd never been allowed.

Two guards flanked the wide door. At my approach, they stiffened. One stepped forward quickly and pulled it open. A rush of warmth met me from the two fireplaces that blazed at either end of the windowless chamber, their smoke curling into the vaulted ceiling. The air smelled of smoke and liquor. I stepped in.

Four men were around the massive oak table. None of them turned. Their focus was on the large, worn map of Landore with wooden markers scattered across the landscape. I lingered inside the door with my hands curled behind my back.

"Your Majesty." Lieutenant Revel's voice rang out. "Your men are stationed in every village," he said, moving a group of red wooden figures toward the western edge of the map. "The villagers are contained, and daily searches continue."

My father rubbed his chin but didn't look west. His eyes were locked on Llycia. "Stop lurking in the shadows. Nobody wants a ghost for a prince." My father's voice boomed with false amusement.

I approached the table, and the three men, still wearing their formal attire, dipped their heads in my direction. There used to be more of them. His council had shrunk. Celeste's father wasn't even present.

The war room doors opened, and Sal slipped inside, taking a post near the wall opposite my line of sight.

"Commander," my father barked. "The rebels in the city?"

Commander Brann adjusted his jacket and cleared his throat. He had been a part of my father's inner council for forever. His silver hair and deepening frown lines were evidence enough. "We've broken up most of the gatherings near the docks, but the citizens are scared.

Some are refusing to work. Trade activity in the hub has dropped significantly."

My father's jaw tightened. "The rebels?"

"They're organized." Brann shifted his weight. "Too organized…every lead we get vanishes."

"You paused," my father snapped. "What aren't you telling me? Who are you protecting?"

"No one, Your Majesty. My allegiance is to you, my king." Brann bowed. "The rebels in the city seem to be working with children."

My father slammed his palms against the table. The pieces jumped. "Children?" he hissed. "You mean to tell me the King's Guard is being outmaneuvered by street urchins?"

Brann swallowed hard but didn't respond.

"Revel. Handle this. Burn the rot out of my city. I don't care what it takes." He looked to Revel who in turn dipped his chin. "I want these threats dealt with!" His gaze cut to me. "Report. The fires. The spies. The prisoners. Tell me something useful."

The fabric around my wrist shifted with the tremble in my hands. I clasped them behind my back. "I've made progress, but I need more time. Three days—"

"Three days?" His jaw snapped tight. Fury surged, then twisted into mocking laughter. "You've had six days. And still you have nothing to show for it. Spies infest my palace. The city burns. And you ask for more time?" He rounded the table toward me. "Do you even understand what's at stake?"

My collar rubbed against my skin. My throat burned.

"Perhaps we should forget our deal altogether," he sneered. "Which is a pity. If you'd brought me a scrap of progress, I was going to let you see your precious pet."

"No," my voice cracked, betraying me. "I just need more time."

"More time." His scoff cut like a blade. "You can't even manage to make an appearance at one of my dinners." He snatched one of the wooden pieces off the table. "The court needs to see us confident. United." He inspected the piece. "They eat, they drink, and they believe we have everything under control." The wooden piece banged against the table in front of me. "Handle these threats." The frustration inside me surged.

Sal shuffled against the wall, a smirk pulling at his lips.

"And which threat would you like me to focus on first?" I asked coldly. "The palace spies? The rebels in the street? Or attending dinners to keep your courtiers clueless?"

The room stilled.

My father moved before I could brace. The crack of his slap split the air, heat blooming sharp across my cheek.

He leaned close, his voice low and full of venom. "You have three days. Three. Or your little pet won't need her hands anymore." He turned away.

I didn't move, didn't breathe.

"Leave." He waved me off like smoke, and I retreated.

"Have we received any verification from that rebel correspondence yet?" my father muttered, barely audible before the doors slammed shut behind me.

I closed my eyes and let out a breath, but it did nothing to steady me. My cheek still burned.

The hallway curved left. John's room sat beyond the next archway.

My steps slowed. I stared at the archway, but pushed on toward my quarters.

A shadow moved at the end of the hall. A guard stepped out in front of me, eyes shifting as though nervous to speak.

"What is it?" I barked.

He flinched. "One of the prisoners...they're unconscious."

"Which one?"

"The woman."

"What happened?" I asked, stepping toward him.

"We...we aren't sure. We found her unconscious when we brought her rations."

"Well, did you call for the Healer?"

"No, sir. I came straight to you first to see what you'd like to do."

"Incompetent," I mumbled with an exhale. "Go call for the Healer."

I changed direction and headed for the dungeon, my head pulsing with every step. The last thing I needed was another failure, another burden to answer for. At the entrance of the dungeon, a guard was slumped in a chair, flipping a coin between his fingers.

"Your Highness!" He bolted upright, knocking the chair over with a bang. "What—ahem—can I do for you?"

"I was told one of our prisoners is unconscious?" I asked, raising a brow.

"Right. Yes, of course." He stumbled over the fallen chair and reached across the table for the key ring. "Would you like me to open it for you?"

"Not necessary." I snatched the keys and stepped past him.

The cell door creaked open, and I braced for the sight of a collapsed body.

Instead, Jules sat cross-legged in the center of the room with her arms folded. When she saw me, the corner of her mouth lifted in a smirk. "Took you long enough," she said, standing and brushing dirt off the front of her trousers.

My brows pulled tight. "You faked it?"

She half-stepped back when I pressed toward her.

"Yes." She lifted her chin. "I needed a way to speak with you."

I exhaled through my nose. Hard. "I don't have time for this." I stepped back to leave.

"You have one day left. You should make time."

My chest tightened. How did she know about my father's deal? "Talk," I ordered.

"Well, I thought we'd start with you," she said, crossing her arms.

"Me?"

"Yes. You're hard to read." She shrugged.

The pressure in my head rose to a pulse. "If this is about mercy, you won't get it."

"I'm not asking for it." Jules straightened. "I wanted to understand what you plan to gain from all this? From sitting back and letting your kingdom be torn apart."

"It's not *my* kingdom."

"No," she said quietly, "but you are the crowned prince." Her voice didn't rise, but her sentiment was like Celeste's, and it pressed on me like a weight. "It will be yours, whether you like it or not."

I stared at the stone wall beyond her, jaw locked. "That's not my choice."

"You think that absolves you?" She stared at me with wide eyes. "Villages are burning. People are hurting. You've seen it. Yet you do nothing."

I gritted my teeth. "You don't know what you're talking about, rebel."

"I think I do." She leaned forward. "I've seen the cracks in your mask. I've seen the rage that leaks out of your control. You're not angry at the rebels. You're angry at yourself."

"Careful," I said, invading her space. "Like you said, your days are numbered."

Her eyes hardened. "So are yours."

Knock, Knock. "Your Highness..."

"What?" I snapped, not breaking my stare.

"It's...umm, the transfer, Your Highness," Oliver said from the doorway. "There's been some complications..."

I released a breath and turned. Oliver was streaked in mud.

"Like I was saying," he pushed a thick, dirt-caked glob of hair from his eyes, "the transfer didn't make it."

I looked past him for a window, a candle, something to tell me the time. My mouth opened to demand answers, but the faint sound of fabric behind me stopped the words.

I pivoted. Jules's hands were clasped behind her back. My eyes narrowed. She was hiding something.

"Your Highness?" Oliver asked, urgency rising.

"I'm coming," I muttered, stepping out, but not before flicking one last glance over my shoulder. Jules held my gaze—and smiled.

Her smile haunted me more than my father's slap.

CHAPTER 20

Talia

THE SOUND OF OARS striking water grew louder and was paired with a low, rhythmic moan that set every nerve in my body on edge. Raph's hand found mine, rough and steady, pulling me into formation with Nadav and Hafsa. The four of us stood shoulder to shoulder, watching the dark mass on the water swell larger with every stroke. Dawn pressed faint gray into the sky, bringing more light across the waves.

"It's not flying any colors," Nadav muttered, eyes narrowing.

Hafsa's tone was sharp, certain. "Pirates."

Raph's grip around my hand tightened, Hafsa adjusted her stance, and Nadav released a low breath. My stomach dropped. I wanted to scream that we needed to turn around, but the ship was three times the size of ours. Outrunning them was impossible.

"I'm sorry," Raph whispered, his voice taut.

"It's not over. We've gotten out of worse." I tried to sound hopeful, but the shake in my voice betrayed me.

"I will die trying to keep you safe." He tightened his hold on my hand.

My throat tightened. "It won't come to that."

A sharp clang rang through my ears. I pulled back as something crashed onto the deck two body lengths away from us, echoing the same sound I'd just heard. A large metal hook skidded across the boards, a rope trailing behind it. The line snapped taut, dragging the hook to the ship's railing where it caught with a jarring thud. The deck lurched under the sudden weight.

Ten men vaulted the rail, swords flashing in the growing light.

Raph's arm came up, protective, as Nadav and Hafsa moved into defensive stances.

The pirates were older, with features that marked them unmistakably as Landorian. I had assumed they were from the other kingdoms.

"Raph," I whispered, tugging on his arm.

He pulled me closer.

My heart pounded erratically against my chest as they closed the distance.

"Drop your weapons," one barked, pointing his sword. The others raised theirs in unison.

Raph was the first to withdraw his sword and drop it. Nadav and Hafsa followed, though every line of their bodies stayed coiled.

One of the pirates zeroed in on me and a lopsided grin formed across his face. "You too, gorgeous," he said, taking a step in my direction.

Raph stepped protectively in front of me. I slipped the dagger from my waistband.

"Hands behind your back!" the same pirate as before ordered. He seemed to be in charge.

Raph dipped his head and moved his hands behind him. I followed.

Pirates with rope stepped forward.

Rough hands grabbed my wrists and the smell of rancid body odor consumed me. It was Lopsided Grin. I stepped away, but he wrapped his hand around my stomach pulling me against his chest.

"It's been too long since I've held a woman in my arms," he said, breathing down my neck.

I squirmed uncomfortably. Raph's face twisted into pure rage.

A gruff laugh came from another pirate to my left. "Looks like you're out of practice, Ronan."

"I'd watch that filthy tongue of yours, unless you want to wake up without it," Ronan answered back, and pain shot through my side as his fingers dug in, my knees giving way.

"Enough!" The pirate who had been barking the orders moved his sword in Ronan's direction. The other pirates surrounding us straightened their backs, and, thankfully, Ronan released his hand from my stomach and worked on tying my wrists.

"You're welcome to whatever we have," Raph said through clenched teeth to the head pirate.

"There's only one thing we need."

His eyes found mine. My stomach plunged, cold and hollow.

"Bring her across. Throw the rest overboard," he ordered.

Ronan grabbed me, separating me from Raph and the others. The blood drained from my face. I screamed. "No! Stop!"

Raph and I locked eyes through the chaos. Fear covered his whole face, but it wasn't for himself. We lost eye contact as the distance between us grew, but I could still see him push against the pirate who was leading him to the side of the ship. The pirate fell.

Raph cut through Nadav's ropes and then Hafsa's. They were fighting back.

Ronan released his hold on me and took a step toward the fighting. This was my chance to do something. To fight back. Taking a deep breath, I stepped closer to him and threw my head forward, straight for his nose. A crunch and a guttural groan told me I hit my mark.

I slammed my right heel into his foot and waited for him to lose balance before I kicked him square in the chest. He fell to the ground.

I paused, stunned I'd managed it. He stirred, groaning, and I bolted toward the circle of fighting.

Metal striking metal rang through the air, but I couldn't see Raph, Nadav, or Hafsa. There were about ten pirates circling around them. I worked my way around the circle, trying to find an opening. A small one appeared, leading straight to Hafsa who was moving with a speed that seemed impossible.

I shot forward.

Pain radiated through my shoulder as I was thrown to the ground. Ronan loomed over me, with blood dripping from his nose and fury twisting his features.

I scooted back, trying to put distance between us. But he grasped my forearm and jerked me up. Another sharp stab of pain shot through my shoulder, the same one that had been dislocated.

With my feet underneath me I kicked and pulled. I felt like a feral cat, forgetting all the training Adira and Hafsa had taught me.

"Enough!" A voice like a whip cracked over the ship.

Everyone froze.

A fierce but beautiful woman stood at the helm of our ship, framed against the fading moonlight. Her dark eyes scanned the area and narrowed when they landed on me. She tightened her grip on the railing and then moved away to descend the stairs.

My eyes flicked to Raph and the others. Their chests heaved and sweat dripped from their faces. They still stood in the middle of the circle with their swords raised, but they were severely outnumbered.

"Captain, we trie—"

The woman put up her hand.

She moved straight for me, her right hand coming to rest on the pommel of the sword attached to her hip. The wind blew her dark hair behind her. It was thick and coarse, pulled into rough locks that looked like braids.

There was something wild and dangerous about her.

She stopped in front of me, her eyes dragging over me. "So you're the princess the kingdom's been thrown upside down for," she said, voice low and unimpressed.

I straightened, ignoring the pounding in my shoulder. "What do you want?"

She didn't answer. Instead, her gaze landed on Raph, Nadav, and Hafsa, still surrounded by blades. "I have everything I want," she said, flicking her gaze back to me. "Even if we had to wait over a week to get it."

Understanding dawned on me, they'd been waiting for me. "How did you know?" I asked.

She circled me. "But it was worth it. The price on your head will keep us happy for months, won't it boys?" She extended her arms out, addressing the surrounding pirates.

They grunted their agreement.

"Who sent you?" I asked.

Her arms dropped. A wicked grin pulled at her lips. "You're not that smart for a princess." She tilted her head. "Who would pay handsomely to have you captured?"

My breath caught. "King Madden," I whispered.

"Maybe she does have a brain after all," the captain laughed. "It's time for you to head back to your little palace, princess."

I was ready to bargain, to find a way to sway these pirates. I opened my mouth, but before a word could leave it Raph shouted my name and her fist connected with my temple.

Darkness covered me.

CHAPTER 21

Raph

"RAPH." A VOICE, SOFT and close, was the first thing I registered followed by the sound of wood groaning, the slap of water, and the steady beat of a drum, which beat in time with the headache behind my eyes. My face throbbed like I'd gone a few rounds with a brick wall. The air was damp and salty. The stench of sweat, mold, and rot settled in my throat.

"Raph, wake up," the same voice said. Cool fingers brushed my forehead, slicing through the fog of pain.

My right eye cracked open. Everything blurred. Shapes swam in and out of focus until one came into view: Talia.

She leaned over me. A bruise swelled along her cheekbone, but her eyes were wide with worry.

"Hey," I croaked, my throat raw.

Her shoulders sagged in relief. "You're okay."

A groan escaped before I could answer. I realized I was lying on the floor with my head in her lap. She kept brushing her fingers through my hair. I turned my head slowly. Iron bars framed the cell, thick with rust. A single lantern swayed in the corner, barely enough light to see. The floor rocked gently under me. We weren't on our ship anymore.

"Nadav?" I rasped.

She nodded over her shoulder. "He and Hafsa are still unconscious, but they look to be in better condition than you."

I pushed myself upright with a wince, pain flaring up my side. Talia helped me lean against the side of the ship. "Yeah, I don't think they liked how I retaliated after the captain knocked you out."

Her hand grazed her cheekbone. "What happened?"

"I lunged for the captain," I muttered. "Didn't get far before her men were on me. There were too many of them." I pressed my hand against my side and inhaled sharply.

Talia lowered her gaze. Her mind reeling about something.

Behind her, Nadav stirred. A low grunt echoed as he rolled onto his side. Hafsa moved next.

"Hafsa?" Nadav called out.

"I'm here, my dear." Hafsa reached her hand out to him.

They helped each other to a sitting position and assessed one another's injuries. Their foreheads touched, and they whispered something too low for me to hear. Their eyes finally landed on us.

"How long—"

"I just woke up." I cut Nadav off.

A heavy clang echoed above. The ceiling trembled faintly. Talia stiffened beside me. Footsteps descended the stairs.

Two pirates stepped into view behind the bars. I curled my hands into fists. One of them was Ronan and blood still crusted his crooked nose. A small smile teased Talia's lips. The other pirate was lean with a blade at each hip.

"Well, well," Ronan sneered. "Sleeping beauty's awake." His gaze narrowed at Talia.

She didn't move. She simply met Ronan's glare with a sharp one of her own.

Ronan stepped forward, hands wrapping around the bars of the cell.

"Ronan," the second pirate drawled. "Captain wanted us to check on her cargo, that's it."

Ronan rattled the bars. Talia jumped beside me.

"Looks like they're all breathing," he said with a laugh.

The lean pirate grunted. "Good. We can't miss out on the pay because one of 'em dies in transit."

Ronan snorted. "If we don't get paid, Captain's going to have a mutiny on her hands."

"Careful what you say." The lean pirate's eyes flicked toward the stairwell. "Let's go," he said, but Ronan lingered.

"Wait 'til you see what's waiting for you in Llycia, Princess," he said, shoving off from the bars with a twisted grin.

There was a moment of silence, as if none of us could comprehend our new situation.

"Those pirates..." Talia spoke. "They were waiting for us."

"For a whole week," I added.

"How could they have known?" Hafsa asked. A bruise on her cheek was already darkening.

"How did Madden know?" I asked, unable to hide my frustration about it all.

"Someone back in Aydencia had to have—"

"No." I said over Talia, sharper than I meant to. "There aren't any spies in Aydencia. No one has loyalty to Madden." But as the words left my lips doubt had already crept in.

"No one might have allegiance to him," Nadav spoke slowly, "but it was obvious some Aydencians were against the idea of a war."

Talia inhaled. "The protesters."

"They wouldn't..." I said, biting my lip.

"You'd be surprised what deals some people will make to ensure they get what they want," Hafsa finished.

Talia's eyebrows pinched together. "So you're saying maybe some of those protesters in Aydencia made contact with King Madden and informed him we would be leaving? And they did this in hopes of what?"

"To not have a full-blown war," I said, rubbing my fingers through my hair. I winced and dropped my hand from the pain.

Talia glanced at me with concern and then looked back at Nadav and Hafsa. "I still don't understand."

"The king wants you," Hafsa explained. "If they could offer you, maybe he would agree to some sort of peace treaty."

"He would never," she said.

"No," I agreed. "But they were probably willing to take their chances."

Nadav and Hafsa nodded their heads in agreement.

The silence returned, this time heavier.

Talia shifted, her arms wrapping around her knees. "What do we do?" she asked. Her head dipped, hair spilling forward. "I can't go back to him." Her voice cracked. "I can't..." Her breaths came quick and shallow.

I looked at Nadav and Hafsa. They gave me a small nod and turned their gaze away, giving us space.

I shifted directly in front of Talia, blocking out the rest of the cell. "Look at me," I said softly.

Her eyes lifted. Wide. Frightened.

"You're not in this alone. We'll figure it out."

"How?" Her voice was tense. "We're locked up, outnumbered, and being dragged back to King Madden."

Her words were like a blow to my chest. Our chances were basically nothing, but I had to believe there'd be a way we'd survive this.

"There'll be an opening, we just have to be ready for it." I reached out and tucked a piece of hair behind her ear. "Don't give up. I need you to fight."

She stared at me for a long beat, her chest still rising and falling too fast. "Okay," she whispered.

I brought my hand to the nape of her neck.

She leaned in. My breath stilled. It would be too easy to kiss her.

I pulled back, "Talia..."

"It's fine," she said quickly, retreating herself.

"No," I caught her wrist before she could fully pull away. "I meant what I said, I will follow you to the ends of this kingdom and the next. " I exhaled, "What I'm trying to say is...I choose you."

Her voice was a whisper. "Choose me?"

I nodded, heart pounding and the fear of rejection clawing up my throat. "Yes. Whatever comes, whatever the future brings, I want to face it with you." The words I'd feared for so long left me lighter, like exhaling something I'd been holding onto for years. I'd spent too long keeping it buried, convincing myself I didn't deserve her. But I couldn't keep it in anymore. She needed to know how I felt, even if she didn't feel the same.

I took in every one of her features, soaking in her beauty. "I choose us."

We hovered there, the ship creaking around us, the air heavy with salt and quiet. I closed the space between us slowly, giving her every chance to pull back. But she stayed. Her breath mingled with mine.

I lowered my lips to meet hers.

Her mouth was soft, hesitant at first, but then she pressed into me with quiet certainty, answering the question I hadn't dared ask out loud.

Heat pulsed through my chest. And for a moment, there was no prison. No pirates. No King. Just us.

I didn't know how, but I was determined to save her from it all. Our story would not end before it even started.

CHAPTER 22

Kasper

THE WAX BLED OFF the candle's edge and pooled on the table. The ink in the report blurred. I blinked hard, feeling the burning sensation in the back of my eyes, and tried to focus again on the report: Looted storefronts. Two more buildings set ablaze. A guard killed trying to break up a mob near the city gate. The unrest wasn't slowing. It was spreading.

And it wasn't just rebels anymore. Villagers were joining in. Fueling it. Feeding on it. At this rate, the entire city would need to be locked down. Only those who resided in the city would be allowed to stay.

My time was running out, again. With the growing unrest in the city I was left with no time to question the prisoners and servants. I had two days. The page crinkled in my hand. I set it down and pushed away from the desk. I had one last card in my hand and I needed to finally play it. I'd been putting it off, but that wasn't an option anymore. It was time to take a lesson out of my father's playbook.

I yanked the door open. A guard stood on the other side with a raised fist.

"Your Highness." He bowed. "The king demands your presence in the throne room immediately."

His timing was perfect like always.

At a brisk walk, I made my way down the too familiar route to the throne room. Two guards reached for the doors the moment they saw me. They creaked open, without fail, before I stepped into the half-filled room.

It seemed my father had summoned his court, but many were missing. The nobles in attendance kept close to one another and whispered behind gloved hands. Their faces turned as I entered. They bowed, but behind their eyes I could easily see a blanket of fear. Celeste's gaze burned into me from next to her father, away from her usual posse.

I looked toward the throne. But my father was at the base of the dais, pacing. The sword at his hip clinked softly with every turn. His crown, heavy with rubies, tilted slightly on his head. His fingers twitched by his side. His wide eyes landed on me, and he stopped.

My heart rate spiked. I bowed and took my spot at the side of the dais.

He turned toward the crowd and lifted a single hand. The whispers in the room lulled.

"All of you know why you're here." His voice cut through the room like a blade. "There are times when a field grows wild, overrun with rot and disease."

Silence.

"It must be burned. If it isn't, the infestation spreads."

He paced again. A quick glance to the closest nobles reiterated what I was thinking. Something was wrong for my father to behave so unsettled.

"I've been merciful. I've given it time. But I've only come to see how my mercy has given traitors space to multiply. That ends tonight."

A hush fell. My fingers curled into my palms.

He flicked his hand in the air. The throne room doors opened. It was hard to make out the figures coming through, but the rattle of shackles and clang of armor revealed enough. The doors closed with a final boom. I could then make out the line of prisoners being led in. My gaze trailed past some servants I had interrogated, a few guards, and beside them were the two rebels. Or I suppose, one rebel, and Princess Talia's friend. She was standing protectively close to John. I went to look away, but froze. There, crammed between more servants, was Lliana.

A strange, sharp pressure pressed against the inside of my ribs. Her head hung low, hiding her face, and her hair, once so soft I could spend hours running my fingers through it, was now tangled and matted to a point that almost made her unrecognizable. She was thinner too. The kind I had only seen on prisoners who we held for years, or in the dark corners of the city where some sit, begging.

I forced my jaw to stay locked, but my hand flicked to my pommel.

The king spread his arms. "Behold, what happens when infestation goes unchecked."

He motioned to two guards, and they dragged three trembling servants to the center. One looked no older than fifteen. I had marked him for further questioning because I knew he could have allegiance to the rebels. But he reminded me even more of myself at fifteen, as he stood before the same man who stood over me. My attention landed on another servant with fiery red hair; she was one of Princess Talia's maids.

"Those before you helped feed the rot and spread the poison of the rebels from the inside. It's time we cut that rot out."

A quick whistle followed by a gleam of light. It took a moment to comprehend that the sword by the king's side was dripping blood onto the marble. It was the thud of a servant's body that made clear what had happened.

Gasps followed. Another thud, but the servant boy still stood, shaking. A commotion in the crowd showed some noble lady had fainted. A few were trying to help her up, but most watched on, frozen. As if staying perfectly still would save them from the hunter in front of them.

The king motioned to a guard, who pushed the servant boy forward. My hand closed tighter around my pommel. The boy's body collapsed before he could flinch. Blood streamed across the floor, winding into the cracks of the white marble.

John's voice cut through the silence, quiet but unshaken. "If you kill all your subjects, who will be left for you to rule?" His gaze was steady, sharper than any blade. He did not cower, and that, more than words, made the king's grin falter.

"Ah yes...the princess's so-called father." The king prowled toward John. "This man kept our dear princess locked away for years. He kept her from us! He probably filled her head with all sorts of rebellious thoughts."

John didn't flinch.

"You probably handed her to the enemy yourself," the king hissed.

The room was still with anticipation. John's gaze never wavered, nor did he shrink back. "You may believe whatever story you like, but the truth will win out."

The king's face flushed dark, eyes burning. His hand snapped up, clamping around John's throat.

"Stop!" Jules screamed, lunging forward, her shackled hands striking at the king's arm. He swatted her aside like she was nothing. She crashed against the floor. The blond rebel surged forward, but was yanked back by a guard.

The king looked between them with a knowing look that made my stomach turn.

His blade plunged.

The sound was wet and final. John staggered, then fell, crimson blooming under him.

Iron coated the inside of my mouth.

Jules screamed and crawled her way to John's body while the blond rebel fought against the guard still holding him.

"Kill the rest of them," the king said, turning his back on the line of prisoners who began to cry out and beg for mercy.

Everything inside me tore open. I took a step forward, but froze as my eyes flicked to Lliana. Her sunken eyes were fixed on me. The guard closest to her hadn't moved. What was he waiting for?

"Our rebel prisoners," the king announced, strolling toward Jules and the blond rebel. "Alas, my son was inadequate at cracking either of you. But perhaps he was pursuing from the wrong angle." His eyes bounced from me to Lliana. "I applaud your stubbornness," he circled them, "But my patience wanes thinner by the second. Answer now, and you can save them." He threw a hand to the other prisoners being held by guards.

Silence.

I stared at Lliana, calculating the distance. The guard was closer. She was out of my reach and that realization burned me alive.

The king stepped toward Jules, tightening his grip around his sword.

Gil broke. His voice was hoarse, desperate. "There's an opening through the Northern Mountains. You can only reach it by boat." My father's lips curled. Gil continued, "It's not visible to the naked eye, unless you know what to look for."

My father's smile deepened. "Well, I guess you'll be the one to lead us there." He handed his sword to a nearby guard and rolled his shoulders back, extending his arms out to his court, smiling benevolently. "We are one step closer to squashing this epidemic. Soon we shall return to our peace and continue to prosper. That I solemnly promise to you."

Some guards and nobles cheered in response, but not all. Half looked pale, their eyes wide and backs straight.

My father turned to me. Blood was splattered along his jacket and face. "If you don't want her to be next," he nodded to Lliana, "you better prove yourself." He stepped closer. "You can imagine my surprise when my informants told me they believed the rebels had a soft spot for each other." His gaze shifted to Lliana, then back to me. His eyes darkened. "I thought you knew what to do when your enemy reveals a soft spot." Disappointment dripped from his every word.

"I do, Father." The word was like ash on my tongue. "I was planning to inform you once I had extracted the exact location of the rebel camp."

His hand clasped around my shoulder. The weight of iron shackles disguised as a father's touch. "Well," he said, "now you have the chance to lead me there yourself. You will bring me to the doorstep of my enemy."

His eyes searched mine. I buried every emotion I felt deep down, but the blurry red liquid over his shoulder filled my vision. I forced myself to nod. He smiled.

Lliana's guard yanked her forward, her feet sliding through John's blood.

He watched me, waiting for the crack. My lungs burned, my jaw locked, but my eyes betrayed me. I looked away first.

CHAPTER 23

Talia

LIGHT STABBED THROUGH THE sack, blinding me as the wagon door screeched open. I flinched, my bound wrists pulling against the rope. My pulse roared in my ears and the sack over my head trapped every breath. I was suffocating. Something shifted beside me. A scrape of boots against the wood.

"Raph," I called out through a shallow breath.

"It will be okay," he called back, but his voice was growing distant.

A hand yanked me from the wagon. My legs buckled as I hit the ground, my boots scraping against uneven stone. Cobblestone. I struggled to stay upright. My chest tightened. I didn't need to see. I knew exactly where we were.

The palace.

Someone brushed against my side for a fleeting second, and I told myself it was Raph, needing it to be him.

A door slammed shut. "Let's go get our pay." The Captain's voice rang out close by, followed by a chorus of agreement.

The hand wrapped around my arm pulled me forward. The sack rubbed against my face, and only the shuffle of feet and distant hum of movement reached my ears. The air had changed as well. The hint of smoke I had been smelling since we arrived in Llycia intensified. There was no denying it. My breaths became short. Something wasn't right.

My toe hit something hard and I pitched forward.

The grip on my arm tightened and pulled up, warning me to take a step. Awkwardly, I progressed up stairs, my shoulder burning from being yanked and pulled.

I wanted to call out to Raph and make sure he was still beside me. To feel a little bit of comfort. But my voice wouldn't work. My throat was raw and tight.

We stopped. A body bumped into me.

"Raph?" I whispered.

Whoever it was didn't answer, but they pressed against me.

"Tell His Majesty we've come to collect," the Captain said directly in front of me. "We have what he's been searching for."

No one responded, but the sound of doors grinding on their hinges told me enough. My body screamed at me to turn and run. That whatever I did, I couldn't walk through those doors. The hand pressed me forward. It pushed harder when I dug my heels in.

The stone floor amplified our footfalls.

I tried to reassure myself that this wasn't like last time, but all I could feel was horror and panic. In my mind I pictured what would be in front of me and how far we were to...

The throne room.

My knees buckled as another set of doors opened. A cry slipped my lips as my shoulder was wrenched forward.

I tried to count each step, but my pulse roared in my ears. The stone beneath my feet felt colder, the air heavier. The sound of low whispers pulled my attention. Courtiers. I could picture their eyes glued to me, watching my every movement.

A familiar scent followed—blood.

I nearly doubled over. I trembled, waiting, knowing any moment I would be face to face with the man of my nightmares.

The sack was ripped off.

I blinked, trying to clear my vision.

The throne was straight in front of me.

I stared at its base.

"Who are you?" The captain's voice was sharp.

I flicked my gaze up.

It wasn't him. It wasn't King Madden.

A man, younger than the king, with a dark beard sat on the throne. His back pressed against the velvet, shoulders rigid. There was something cruel and uncertain about his face.

"Well?" The captain stepped forward. "Where is King Madden?"

My gaze darted across the room trying to make sense of it all. Courtiers lined the sides, but there were far fewer of them than before. Whispers stirred. I scanned their faces, recognizing a few of them. I stopped on one familiar face that was closest to the dais.

Celeste. Her chin lifted as our eyes locked. She looked exactly the same, except for the fact she was alone. There weren't any of the other ladies around her, not even Philipa. I scanned the crowd again—

"My business is with King Madden," the captain snapped. "No one else."

The bearded man rose and descended the dais. He stopped at the base, meeting the captain's stare with a flat, unreadable expression.

"I'm afraid His Majesty is not available."

"Not available?" she echoed. "He seemed pretty available when he hired us over a week ago. We aren't leaving until we get paid." She stepped toward him, placing her hand on the pommel of her sword.

The man matched her step. "I have no agreement with you."

Around me, the pirates stirred, hands twitching toward weapons. The grip on my arm loosened. I caught Raph's eye. He gave the barest tilt of his head toward the wall. Two guards stood there. I scanned the room again. At least ten guards total.

"And what power do you have here?" The captain was inches from the man's face.

A voice cut through the room. "This is Regent Revel," boomed Celeste's father, striding forward from the crowd. "And you shall treat him as such."

My gaze shot to the man again, Regent Revel. He still stood at the base of the dais, but now that I looked more closely, I saw it. A crown. Not the jewel-encrusted one King Madden wore, but a simpler circlet of burnished silver, resting above his brow like a placeholder.

The captain shifted her weight backward.

"Regent?" I mumbled under my breath. Raph gave me a side-glance. I searched the faces in the room. They were a mix of fear and triumph. There had been a power shift. But how? And where was King Madden?

"You can either leave on your own," Revel said, raising a hand in signal, "or be forcibly removed." Six guards moved from the edges of the room, encircling the pirates.

"Do you even realize who we've captured?" the captain asked, throwing her arm behind her in my direction.

Revel's gaze landed on me. Hard and unyielding. "I have no use for some rumored princess—"

Small gasps trickled throughout the room. Celeste's father stepped in close and whispered something in Revel's ear.

"We will take the prisoners," Revel said, straightening from Celeste's father. "You may leave."

"Like I said," the captain replied tightly, "not without our pay."

"That's your decision. Guards."

The captain and the five other pirates in front of us withdrew their swords at the same time the six guards advanced with their own swords raised.

"This is your last chance." Revel withdrew his own and pointed it directly at the captain. "Leave."

The captain's eyes narrowed. She looked to her men, to the guards, then back to Revel. Finally, she lowered her sword.

"Tell King Madden we'll be back for what's ours." She turned on her heel, and the other pirates followed. None of them looked in our direction as they walked by.

"If he makes it back." The words were low, but I heard them clearly. My focus snapped back to Revel.

His stare was already fixed on me. I'd been expecting to be delivered to King Madden, not this Regent Revel who'd been put in place by who knows who. I had no idea where I stood with him. He looked at me as if I were a pebble in his path, something to be kicked aside.

"Take them to the dungeons," he ordered, looking away from me.

The guards moved fast. Cold hands closed on my arms. I didn't fight, but my legs barely moved. They felt like lead.

We were escorted out of the throne room and down a narrow corridor, deeper into the palace. I tried to piece it together, Revel, King Madden, the missing nobles, but nothing made sense. It was obvious something had happened, but what? We descended some stairs and the air grew damp, constricting my lungs. I tried to tell myself this was different. I wasn't alone and King Madden was nowhere in sight. But every footfall made my stomach twist.

The guards cut our bindings and shoved us into one cell, slamming the door. With the latch of the lock something inside me snapped.

"What was that?" My voice came out sharp, too loud for the small space. "What is going on?"

Nadav stood next to Hafsa, gently inspecting the raw marks on her wrists. Raph faced the door, his shoulders tight.

"Who even is this Revel?" I paced three steps, pivoted, and crossed back. "Why is he on the throne? Where is King Madden? Prince Kasper? Where are Jules, Gil, and my father?" My voice broke.

Raph turned, but no one answered me.

I pressed the heels of my palms into my forehead. My breath came quick and shallow. "None of this makes sense," I muttered.

The stone floor felt like it was shifting under my feet. I backed into the corner of the cell, the wall cold against my spine. My hands slid to my hair, pushing it back out of my face.

Raph crossed the space in two long strides, his hands gently landing on my shoulders. His touch grounded me.

"We'll figure it out," he said quietly.

I closed my eyes and tried to pull air into lungs that felt tight as fists. More than anything I wanted to believe Raph, but the endless questions clawed at me. Revel. Celeste's father. The missing nobles. A hall that smelled like old smoke and fresh blood. "What if we can't this time?" The words spilled out of me. "Everything we try always seems to go wrong."

Raph didn't argue. His silence said enough.

Nadav's voice broke in, low. "Revel reminds me of a warrior, not some diplomat seeking power." Raph dropped his hands as we turned to look at Nadav. "What I mean is the crown sits on his head because someone put it there."

"Celeste's father," I said. "He's always been after more power."

Raph's jaw worked. "Can we use that? Buy us some leverage?"

My brows pinched together. "What do you mean?"

"Showing him you'd be an asset to help legitimize his power grab," Raph answered.

"You mean convince him that the lost princess will help placate the people of Landore?" I could see where Raph was going. Me stepping back into my role as princess. The thought burned heavily in the pit of my stomach.

Hafsa stepped closer, her expression soft and steady. "There is a difference between saving yourself and selling your freedom. Just be sure you count the cost." Her gaze fixed on me. "I know what it feels like when the walls close in. But walls can be broken down. You just have to find the right angle to see the crack."

Raph's hand gently reached for mine, anchoring me to the fact that I wasn't alone in this. I stared at our hands. The old fear lapped at my ankles, but so did something else. Resolve.

"I'm not going to be anyone's puppet," I said. "Not Madden's. Not Revel's. Not anyone's. If I speak with Celeste's father, it will be on our terms. And the first term is simple." I lifted my chin. "We get out and find my father, Jules, and Gil."

Hafsa's mouth curved up, small and fierce. Nadav nodded his head, like a warrior taking orders.

Raph's gaze held mine. "I'm with you."

His words mirrored what he told me on the pirate ship. That he chose me. I hadn't answered him then. I hadn't been ready. But now, with my future uncertain, I knew my answer. My heart drummed against my chest.

"I choose you too," I whispered. "Whatever waits for us, Revel, Madden, the whole kingdom, I want you by my side. I want the chance to fight for a future...with you."

Raph's brows drew tight as his gaze intensified. Something unspoken passed between us. His hand tightened around mine. "Then we start with an audience with Celeste's father. We will find their weak point and exploit it," he said with a new sense or urgency.

I nodded, my pulse steadying. My whole life I had looked to others to decide my place, my worth, my future. No more. Whatever game Celeste's father thought he was playing, whatever cage this regent tried to build around me, I would not be their pawn. I would carve my own path. I would fight for the life I wanted.

CHAPTER 24

Jules

THE GENTLE SWAY OF the ship rocked me back and forth, a rhythm I hated myself for finding almost soothing. Four days in a barred cell below deck had worn me down. My body moved with the sea whether I wanted it to or not. All hope leaked out of me one wave at a time.

Next to me, Gil sat with his back against the wall, one knee pulled up, his face unreadable. Even his steadiness felt foreign. It had anchored me. Now it made the emptiness inside me louder. Neither of us had spoken since the morning. There was nothing else to say. Every theory, plan, and hope had been picked apart and worn out. The silence between us had grown familiar, as if there was still a stone wall separating us.

Gil broke the silence. "You should try to rest."

"I can't," I muttered, not bothering to explain how every time I shut my eyes I saw John's lifeless body in front of me.

He studied me from the corner of his eye, shadows carved deep beneath them. "It wasn't your fault. John wouldn't—"

My throat burned. "Don't."

"It's not your fault," he pressed, voice low but firm.

"Yes, it is." I faced him. "I was supposed to protect him. I promised Tals—" A sob broke out.

"You did everything in your power to keep that promise."

"And it wasn't enough." I shook my head, letting the tears fall. "It doesn't matter how much I fight back. We won't win this."

His jaw flexed. He looked away, then back at me. "Don't give up. We can't hand them the victory."

"Haven't they already won? We're leading them to Aydencia." The pit inside me only widened, knowing that was my fault as well. "What else can we do?" I whispered.

Gil leaned his head back against the wood, letting out a slow breath. His voice was low, but I heard every word. "Maybe the only fight left is deciding what we're willing to die for."

His words landed like a stone in my gut, but a part of me welcomed them. Before I could ask what he meant, boots thudded down the stairwell.

Neither Gil nor I moved.

Kasper emerged from the shadows, his face caught between the swing of the lantern, light and dark. He stopped outside the bars, hands clasped neatly behind his back.

None of us spoke. The silence pressed in as his eyes flicked over me, then to Gil, and back again. For a moment I thought I saw the smallest fracture in his composure. Guilt? Regret? Something unspoken haunted his features, but when the light moved on him again it was gone.

"What happened in the throne room..." His voice was low. "It shouldn't have happened."

My heart reached for his words that almost sounded sorrowful, but my mind recoiled against them. If he truly meant them, he should've done something to stop any of it from happening.

Before I could open my mouth two guards appeared.

"Your Highness," one dipped his head, "orders?"

Kasper squared his shoulders and his voice turned hard and almost lifeless. "Bring them up." He turned and retreated up the stairs.

"On your feet," the guard barked, as he opened the cell door.

Gil slowly pushed himself up, his movements stiff.

The guard moved deeper into the cell. "You too," he said looking at me.

I remained frozen.

He yanked me up.

"Leave her alone," Gil snapped, but the second guard forced him against the wall and secured his wrists with rope. He didn't fight back, but his glare said he wanted to. Rough hands tied my wrists and shoved me out of the cell.

We were hauled up the narrow staircase, the salty air growing sharper with each step. Light seared across my vision, blinding after days below deck. I squinted against it as we stepped onto the main deck.

Dozens of guards with weapons and grim faces watched as we were led across the slick planks. Wind whipped at my hair. The guard behind me shoved me forward toward the helm, but my focus was to my left where huge, imposing mountains towered over us.

We had reached the Northern Mountains.

The guard led me toward the largest mast near the center of the ship. I flinched as my back hit the mast. Gil was forced to keep moving, the distance between us growing. He peered over his shoulder at me and stopped, he looked almost regretful. The guard shoved him onward.

Splinters bit into my skin as coarse rope wrapped around my waist, anchoring me to the post. I kept my eyes on Gil. He was brought up the stairs to the helm, where a man stood at the wheel, his grip firm despite the soft breeze. By the man's side stood Kasper, rigid and with an unreadable expression.

"Uh," I grunted as the rope squeezed the air out of my lungs.

"Too tight?" The guard smirked to the side of me before walking away.

Kasper's mouth opened, but his words were lost in the wind. His gaze flicked to me and so did Gil's.

My breath stilled.

Gil didn't say anything, he just nodded once. He turned to the man at the wheel, who must have been the captain, and said something.

The captain glanced over at Kasper, uncertain. Kasper gave a subtle nod. With a grunt, he turned the wheel slightly.

The wind caught the sails and the bow shifted, barely, but enough to make the deck groan beneath my feet. The change in direction sent ripples through the crew. Whispers and nervous glances toward the jagged peaks getting closer.

I shifted against the ropes, trying to get comfortable. Small splinters of wood rubbed against my back.

Time dragged, but Gil remained still beside the helm, his arms tied behind him. Not once did his facade drop. He was giving them everything. He was handing over his home to be destroyed, yet he kept the same unreadable expression, calm and detached.

Guilt clawed at my throat, but it was suffocated by the numbness that had taken over.

Movement at the helm drew my attention. Kasper descended the stairs and walked straight toward me. He moved with confidence. My stomach twisted but I refused to cower underneath his stare.

He stopped directly in front of me, hands clasped behind his back. He didn't say anything.

"What do you want?" I mumbled.

His eyes flicked to the ropes binding me, then back to my face.

"Are you just going to stand there silent, doing nothing, like you did as your father murdered innocent people?" There was no emotion in my voice. "Do you think this war will end with peace? That your father will stop once he destroys the rebel camp?"

He looked toward the mountains.

"He won't. He won't be satisfied until all of Landore burns."

He looked at me again. "You think I have a choice?"

"Of course you do."

He didn't answer.

"This is as much your choosing as his. Every death, every village burned, every child orphaned, that's on your head as well."

He stepped back, his face tightening. "You don't get it. You don't understand what he'll do if—"

"I don't care," I said. "You have the power to end this."

The corner of his eye twitched, and his mouth parted like he was going to say something. But he stood there. Silent. Whatever words had risen died behind his clenched jaw. He turned and walked away.

"You're worse than him," I said, my voice taken by the wind.

He didn't look back, but his shoulders seemed to tense. He positioned himself back by the helm.

I dropped my head back against the wooden pole and waited. The wind picked up the closer we got to the mountains, whipping across the deck.

The captain gestured toward the mountains, fear etched across his face.

Kasper stepped closer and gave some sort of command.

The captain looked between Kasper and Gil and shook his head.

Kasper's hand fell to his sword. There was a moment of stillness before the captain shoved away from the wheel. A guard moved beside him at the same moment

Kasper unsheathed his sword and cut straight through Gil's ropes.

Gil stepped to the wheel, placing both hands on it. His eyes flicked to me briefly.

"He is going to kill us," a guard muttered next to me.

"Maybe that's the point," I said, too quietly for anyone to hear. But my words stuck and a knot formed in my throat. What if that was his plan? To take himself, the guards, Kasper, me, all of us, down to save Aydencia?

Anger and betrayal flared hot and fast. He didn't tell me. Didn't even ask me. And after everything, this is how it was going to end.

"Hard port! Hard port!" Gil yelled, as spray hit my face. The crew clung to rails and ropes.

Beneath my anger, something else stirred. My whole life I had carried the weight of my calling, doing what was best for the Hunters. Everything my parents taught me was about sacrifice. It's what leaders did. And this would be a sacrifice that could save all of Aydencia.

My vision blurred, but I couldn't tell if it was sea water or tears.

Shouts from those around me rose over the wind.

My gaze shot to Kasper. His face was pale, lips pressed thin, but his eyes were locked on Gil at the wheel, not the mountain ahead. Gil's eyes remained fixed forward.

Collectively, everyone held their breath for impact.

My stomach turned. Was I ready to die?

No.

The word sparked like a match inside me. No. I wanted to live. To fight. To discover who I could be. I fixed my gaze on Gil, willing him to not do this.

The ship pitched violently. Shouts turned to screams. Someone yelled to brace for impact. But it never came.

The relief around me was audible, but it didn't last long. Gil continued to shout orders at the crew. The passageway we had entered was extremely narrow and this ship was huge, about twice the size of the ship I had been on with Talia. When we first boarded Gil tried to tell them it might not survive the journey, but the captain took great offense to that, and Gil had the swollen eye to prove it.

"Starboard!"

The ship jerked to the right. The guards around me stumbled to the ground as my body slammed against the wooden pole. I couldn't hold back the groan. Gil's eyes instantly found mine. I pressed my lips together firmly, refusing to show any discomfort. He went back to yelling out orders.

I pressed against the restraints and wiggled my shoulders, attempting to release an arm or something. Releasing my breath, I relaxed against the wooden pole. It was pointless. Even if I was free, what difference could I make?

A loud crack filled the air. Wood flew up as the right side of the ship crashed against the mountain's wall, leaving part of the railing broken. It got worse further into the passageway as the ship continued to hit one side of the mountain and the other. I wasn't the only one doubting whether the ship would make it out in one piece. The King's Guard abandoned their duties to cling to parts of the ship for dear life. The other guards, who were more rugged in their appearance, showed a little more confidence while traversing through the narrow passage.

Gil caught my eye and for a brief second I thought I could almost see some form of a smile on his lips before the ship rammed into the side of the mountain again. Maybe he did have a plan in all this?

Within moments the air around me shifted. The ship steadied. The mountains widened. And the guards loosened their holds and began to laugh and shove one another.

But the unease inside me only grew. I was alive, but at what cost? My thoughts went to Talia and the others, hoping they'd be able to get out in time. I blinked hard and kept my eyes on Gil, waiting for this nightmare to be over.

I strained my neck to look behind me, but the pole was too large for me to see anything. However, the distance between the mountains and the ship was growing. I kept my head turned wanting to see a glimpse of what was in front of us.

"What...what is that?"

"That's no rebel camp..." Another said.

"It's a setup." The fear was evident in the last voice.

I turned to find Gil standing with a smug look on his face.

CHAPTER 25

Kasper

WHEN I WAS TEN my father took me to the docks and made me stand beside him as another kingdom's ship burned. He wanted me to learn the sound of desperate men crying out for mercy, for their lives to be spared. Their screams haunted me for weeks. Looking at the rebel city, I heard them again, as if the fire and destruction were already decided.

"Your Highness." The captain's voice cracked. He was in control of the ship again, and his eyes were fixed on the wall of ships guarding the entrance.

My jaw slackened. Whatever came next wasn't going to be pretty. Because this wasn't a camp. This wasn't tents and smoke curling from fires.

This was a city.

Houses were carved into the face of the mountain. Stone bridges arched over different sections creating a maze-like feel. Where I expected filth and tents, there was symmetry and structure. There were shops built at the base. This was permanent.

They hadn't survived, they'd thrived. There had to be thousands of people living there. I squeezed my eyes shut and reopened them. Nothing changed.

My stomach turned to iron. My father planned to burn this place to the ground and expected me to light the match.

"Lower the sails," I said hoarsely.

The captain relayed the order. The deck shuddered as canvas readjusted. I caught the blond rebel's smug grin. I was surprised when he had not led us straight into the face of the mountain. Now I saw this for what it truly was. I shoved him toward the closet guard. "Secure him to the mast with the other prisoner."

The ship groaned. I turned to our rear and saw that my father's ship and three others had made it out so far, but they looked battered. One of them had a chunk missing from the front, but luckily it was high enough that they didn't seem to be taking on water.

I focused back on the line of rebel ships we were fast approaching. They were arranged, oars leveled, hulls braced. They had been waiting for us. They must have had some lookout system in the narrow passageway.

I couldn't help but wonder what my father would be thinking. There was no way he would retreat, not after coming this far and being so close to getting what he wanted for years. But he had to realize this was more than we were prepared for. This was a fortified city, not a little rebel camp hiding in caves.

One of our ships came up on our left and another on our right. They formed a barrier, mirroring the rebel line. We still had the upper hand, our seven compared to their six, but we had no idea how many they had on board or how many would be waiting for us once we hit land.

The ship on our left pulled ahead. My father stood at the rail of it, broad as a storm, his eyes fixed on what lay ahead. I waited, hands clenched around the railing, until he lifted his fist, giving the signal.

"Archers! Ready yourselves!" I ordered.

My father's men got into position around the edges of the ship. Bows were drawn. Upon their movement the ship next to us followed suit.

The captain called out, holding onto the wheel, "Ready the oars!"

The ship increased in speed. I dug my fingernails into the railing until my knuckles went white. The sea sprayed across my face. I felt the old memory return, the scent of burning wood. We were a few hundred yards out. The rebel ship's oars hit the water, rising and falling in perfect unison.

"Steady," I called out. The only response was the slap of oars and the groan of hulls.

The sea was too still. Too quiet.

A scream ripped through the air. It was like a warning bell.

My father's ship crashed through the line. The sound of wood splintering echoed over the water.

"Hold your fire!" I barked, my eyes tracking the gap ahead. Two more rebel ships swerved into place and sealed off the breach.

Our bow crested, crossing directly with theirs.

"Fire!"

A cloud of black arced skyward, but they quickly answered back with a wave of their own. An arrow whizzed right above my head, lodging itself into the wood of the ship. Another clipped the helm. A guard went down screaming.

"Spears!" The captain bellowed.

The oars retracted and the ship slowed. Metal spears slid into place. We veered left toward the rebel vessel closing in. My father's ship mirrored us on the other side. We would hit them from both sides.

"Brace!"

"Fire," I ordered the archers.

The ship bucked. Screams echoed across the length of the deck. I hit the planks hard and rolled. A guard slammed into the railing, grabbing onto a rope line to stop from toppling over the side.

Arrows rained down.

A rebel leaped from their railing with a war cry and landed on our deck. He didn't make it two steps before a blade tore through his chest. Blood splattered on the boards. Another tried to jump but vanished beneath the waves.

The screams, the splintering wood, the blood across the deck—all of it pressed on me, but the weight of my father's expectations was heaviest.

"Push through!" I roared.

"Full speed," the captain echoed.

We tore past the crippled rebel ship. Its hull listed, oars snapped like brittle bones. I scanned the water. My father's ship plowed on, but the one next to him didn't make it through. Their bow was stuck in a rebel's ship. The ring of swords striking could be heard across the water. They had boarded each other. Two ships on my right slipped through, but one dragged in the water. The remaining three were still engaged with rebel ones, it was too difficult to know if they would make it through or not.

My gaze caught the blond rebel tied to the mast beside Jules. He was watching me with the same smug expression. I narrowed my eyes, searching for answers I didn't know the questions to. Jules didn't have the same confidence. She wasn't staring at me. She was looking at the wreckage. Her face was pale, lips pressed into a thin line. There were shattered planks, a broken mast drifting in the water, and a guard coughing up blood as he crawled toward the edge of the ship.

Her despair met my hollow resolve. I looked out toward the rebel camp—no, city. I slammed my teeth together. "Report?" I yelled to Oliver, my second in command.

"Dozen dead. Thirty wounded," he yelled back.

That left us with over two hundred able bodies to fight. I could only assume the other ships had similar numbers. The real gamble was not knowing how many were waiting for us on land.

"Gather the men," I ordered, keeping my gaze ahead. The size didn't change what I had to do. Nothing could.

BOOM.

Water erupted off the port side like a geyser. Everyone ducked. I hit the deck, heart slamming into my ribs. Another boom, but no splash this time, just the thundercrack of wood splitting open.

A mast came down on the ship next to us, tearing part of its other sail with it.

I scrambled up. "What was that?"

"Gunpowder," the captain growled, eyes on a lone rebel ship behind us. "Tro'ishian war tactic. We need to move."

BOOM.

Another shot, but our ship wasn't the target this time. It was on the two ships behind us that had broken free from the line of rebels.

I spun at the men clustered at the rail. "Men," I barked, stealing their full attention. "The moment we touch land, don't stop. Destroy everything in your path. Burn it if you must. We will break the legs of this rebel group and show them the true power of the King's Guard." They turned to one another with smirks across their faces. "We will make them bleed for going against the king!"

Shouts broke, swords raised in answer.

I left the helm as we neared the wooden docks and stopped in front of a young guard. "Don't let them out of your sight," I said, casting a side glance toward Jules and the rebel.

"Yes, Your Highness," he replied with a bow of his head.

Turning from him, I joined the ranks of the men eagerly waiting for the dock. They held their swords raised in one hand and their circular, iron shields in the other. "Keep your shields up, and don't stop pushing forward!" I commanded, unsheathing my own sword and lowering my stance.

Our ship rammed into the dock.

I jumped with the others, sword raised. But the cry in my throat was hollow, an echo of a war cry.

CHAPTER 26

Jules

It happened fast. Too fast.

Screams filled the air along with steel striking steel.

Half the guards followed Kasper off the ship, those who were left shifted their weight from one foot to the other with their swords raised.

A guard moved closer to us. His face was familiar, even under the helmet.

Jacob Martin.

I pressed against the rope restraining me. Jacob didn't look my way. He took up his post near the mast and stood with a wide stance, sword lifted, his knuckles white. Men in armor swarmed the deck. Their breastplates bore tree sigils instead of the king's crest: Aydencians.

Blades colliding, bodies falling, and endless shouting blurred together. Jacob was pulled into the chaos.

A body slammed into the mast near me, blood streaking the wood. "We need to get out of these ropes," I gasped, straining against the bindings.

Gil's voice was maddeningly calm. "Patience."

"Patience? We're sitting ducks!" I twisted harder, panic crawling up my throat.

But before he could answer me an Aydencian warrior stalked toward us with his sword lifted. Once close enough the man raised the sword over his head.

"Gil!" I screamed and squeezed my eyes shut. Suddenly the ropes dropped to my feet, and air rushed back into my lungs.

"What in Landore are you doing tied up on the enemy's ship?" the man asked, unable to keep his laughter down. He shook his head as if he wasn't too surprised.

I stepped out of the ropes, my focus on the fighting around us.

"Oh, you know, trying to keep things interesting. Lend me that?" Gil grinned and reached for the man's bow.

"It will be of more use in your hands," he said, handing it and his quiver to Gil.

All around us, men collided like waves in a storm. Gil swung the quiver over his back, then released an arrow into the neck of one of the King's Guard. A wicked smile played on his lips as he rolled his shoulders back. I couldn't help the sense of jealousy that overcame me, wanting to have my own bow in my hands.

"Your problem, Robert, has always been that you don't know how to relax." Another arrow flew from his bow, lodging itself in the foot of a guard, giving the Aydencian warrior the upper hand to take him down.

"Yeah, yeah." Robert waved his hand at Gil. "You should probably go check in with Alon, they'll need help up the mountain."

Gil gave him a sharp nod, before looking over to me for the first time. I had my back pressed to the mast so I only needed to worry about my front. Thankfully, everyone was preoccupied with the fight in front of them and hadn't noticed Gil and I were free. Gil scanned me over quickly before moving his attention around the ship. He made his way to the right, leaving me alone. The man who had freed us was already in the middle of fighting two sailors. He might not be good with a bow and arrow, but he could hold his own with a sword.

"Gil," I yelled in a harsh whisper, unsure if I should follow or stay put. He didn't turn around. His lack of urgency during all this fighting was eating at my nerves.

The ship rocked as another handful of Aydencians boarded.

Jacob's line of sight landed on me, and he charged.

"You're not going anywhere, Jules," he spat. My pulse rattled in my ears.

"I'd disagree," Gil's voice cut through. He appeared beside me and shoved a bow and arrow in my hands, then stepped between me and Jacob. He danced around Jacob with a short sword drawn, agile and quick, taunting him.

"Fight me properly!" Jacob roared, slashing wildly in the air.

"Are you not having fun?" Gil asked, with a look of shock on his face.

He continued his little dance. Another King's Guard drew his sword and approached the two of them. I released an arrow, only for it to bounce off of his armor. But it had the effect I was hoping for. He found me and changed course. A small tremble from my hand caused me to send the next arrow too wide.

"It looks like we will have to cut this short. Sorry, lad." Gil's voice broke through the ringing in my ears. In my peripheral, he dropped to the floor with a roll and came up behind Jacob. In the same breath, he used the end of his dagger to knock him out.

The guard approaching me remained oblivious to what had happened. My chest tightened. If he got any closer I was done for. I didn't know how to fight. The guard let out a guttural cry and dropped to a knee. I stood staring at the arrow protruding from the guard's thigh.

"Move!" Gil grabbed my arm, hauling me forward.

We ran off the ship, across the planks, dodging fallen bodies as sparks rained from burning buildings. The air was thick with smoke and ash. And screams. So much screaming.

Gil didn't slow. He dragged me toward the burning heart of the city. The cobblestone road we were on bent, and when we reached the corner we finally encountered where the real battle was taking place. Gil pulled me into an alleyway.

"We need to find a place for you to hide," he said, scanning the burning street.

"No." My voice barely sounded like my own. "I'm not hiding."

His jaw clenched. "This isn't the time to be stubborn. You'll die out there."

"I can help."

He hesitated for a heartbeat.

I raised my bow and shot. I struck a guard in the shoulder, breaking up a skirmish nearby. The crease between Gil's eyebrows deepened as he stared at me. "You're serious?" he muttered.

"Yes," I said, grabbing his arm, anchoring myself to him.

The heat from the buildings on fire licked at our backs while cries and metal hitting metal continued to roar in the background. Gil and I stood in the middle of it all with competing wills. I understood why he didn't want someone as inexperienced as me to join in this fight, but I needed to do this, not only for the people of Aydencia but for myself. It was my fight as well.

"Fine," he said tightly. "But if I say run, you run. No arguing."

"Deal," I breathed.

He shoved a spare dagger into my belt and fitted another arrow to his bow.

"Stay close," he ordered, already moving forward.

I swallowed the lump in my throat and followed. We plunged back into the fire.

CHAPTER 27

Talia

TIME PRESSED AGAINST MY chest in the dungeon, making each breath heavier than the last. I couldn't tell if we'd been locked away for one day or many. The air was sour with mildew and something else I didn't want to name. It was like before—except I wasn't alone.

Nadav sat in the corner with one arm braced over his knee, staring at the door like he could will it open. Hafsa leaned against him, resting her head on his shoulder. Raph didn't sit. He alternated between pacing and standing still. He hadn't said a word in hours.

None of us had. What was there to say? We were in the dark about what was happening. No one had come. Not even to give us food. I shifted my weight and pulled my knees to my chest. My cheek brushed the cool stone wall as I leaned back into the corner. They couldn't keep us here forever. Someone had to come.

Groaning metal snapped through the silence, and the door swung open.

Raph moved and shielded the entry. Nadav and Hafsa scrambled to their feet. I remained still with my breath caught in my throat.

Three silhouettes filled the doorway, blurred by torchlight.

Adira stood front and center, arms crossed, and a gleam in her eye. Behind her, Eitan grinned like he'd won something. And beside them, a boy I didn't recognize stood with a hand on the doorframe. He had curly hair and a smirk.

No one moved. My heart stuttered, not wanting to be wrong about what my eyes were seeing.

"Tommy?" Raph asked in a low voice.

The boy's face lit up with a mischievous grin. "If it's a bad time," he said, eyes sweeping the cell, "we can come back."

A low laugh escaped Raph. It sounded more like a release of pressure than actual amusement. He shook his head, stepping forward.

I pushed myself to my feet.

"What are you doing here?" Raph gave Tommy a light punch to the shoulder. "How'd you get in?" He turned to Adira and Eitan.

Nadav and Hafsa followed him out of the cell, blinking into the torchlight.

I lingered for half a second, trying to convince myself this was real and not a trap, before stepping out of the cell. Over the threshold, I looked down the hallway. It was empty. No guards. No approaching footsteps. Something shifted in my chest.

Eitan clapped Raph on the back. "You've looked better." Raph gave him a dry look.

A few feet away, Adira introduced Tommy to Nadav and Hafsa.

Tommy offered them a two-finger salute and a wink, then his gaze landed on me. "And ya," he said, tilting his head, the glint in his eyes unmistakable, "must be the princess we keep havin' to rescue."

His words stung a little, but I shoved those feelings away and stretched out my hand. "Talia."

Tommy took it without hesitation. "Oh, I know." His eyes flicked to Raph. "Heard all abou' ya."

Raph bumped him hard with his shoulder. Tommy grinned wider. I raised my brow as warmth flushed my cheeks.

"It's nice to meet you." I smiled, lowering my hand. "And thanks for rescuing me, again."

"Nothin' to it," Tommy answered with a shrug.

"How did you guys break in?" Raph asked, falling in step with Tommy as we walked down the corridor. "And where are the guards?"

"Don' worry. We got it handled." Tommy said nonchalantly.

Raph shot him a look and turned to Adira and Eitan.

"The whole city was on the edge of a full-blown rebellion when we arrived," Adira said.

Eitan shook his head. "Riots. Fires…"

My eyes widened. "How?" I asked.

Tommy crossed his arms and puffed his chest. "The Shades have been busy."

I furrowed my brow. "Why didn't King Madden stop it?"

"He tried. Him and his Wraith. But once the spark caugh' it couldn' be put out." Tommy's grin dropped. He rubbed the back of his neck. "Can' take all the credit though. The idea came from some rebel in the palace."

I halted at the base of the stairs. Raph's look had my stomach twisting.

"Are there other prisoners?" I asked, breathless. Everyone else turned to look at me. "We need to find Jules, Gil, and my father."

Adira's gaze dropped. "They're not here," she said, readjusting a knife on her belt. "We've checked every cell."

"He must have hidden them elsewhere," I insisted.

"Someone will know where they are. We could ask a servant or guard," Hafsa offered.

"I just hope whoever this Regent Revel is, that he hasn't done something with them," I said, unable to shake the feeling that they weren't in the palace anymore.

"What's going on with that?" Raph asked, jutting his chin out toward the top of the stairs. "Where's Madden?"

Eitan's face turned grim. "Word is, he declared war. That he and a fleet of ships are on their way to Aydencia right now."

For a beat, no one responded.

My mouth gaped open. "We have to help!"

Eitan shook his head. "We wouldn't make it in time. Besides, they've been preparing for this for years."

"That's impossible." Raph rubbed his face. "How could Madden know the location?"

"Someone must have finally divulged it," Eitan said.

Raph shook his head. "No one would do that."

I placed my hand on his shoulder. "The protests? Pirates?"

Tommy's eyes gleamed with curiosity. "Pirates? Wha' trouble ya been gettin' into, Raphy?"

I curled my lips under, trying to stop from smiling about Raph's nickname.

Raph ignored him. "No. They didn't want a war. The last thing they'd do was bring Madden to our doorstep."

"True. But then who?" I asked.

"Ya know. Ya can ask them yourselves." Tommy looked up the stairs.

"We have them contained in the throne room," Adira explained.

"Who?" I asked, nodding my head forward and taking the first step up.

"Guards. Nobles. And that Revel guy," Adira said over her shoulder.

"We've taken control of the palace." Though I couldn't see Tommy's face, his glee was evident.

Raph scoffed. "The three of you?"

Tommy shrugged. "We migh' 've had some help."

We continued through the halls. Endless questions ran through my mind, keeping me silent.

Everyone pulled back when we approached the double doors, making room for me to step forward. The air felt razor-thin.

I peered over at Raph. He moved directly behind me, offering me the support I desperately needed. I inhaled, casting a glance at Eitan and Adira. There was no sign of fear or worry about what was behind these doors.

I exhaled and pushed them open.

The throne room was packed with people, some armed with pitchforks and others with drawn swords.

They surrounded a cluster of captured guards and nobles in the middle of the room.

I stepped inside. And every head turned.

I scanned the faces in the room. There were people from every calling, a handful of palace servants, and a scattering of nobles.

My breath caught.

Lady Astrid, Lady Marie, and Lady Olivia stood amongst the crowd. Their silk dresses were wrinkled and dirty, and their hair fell loose from once-perfect styles. Their faces lit up as soon as they saw me, their smiles bright and desperate all at once. I offered a smile back, my heart twisting. Another familiar face pulled my attention. Beyond my old ladies-in-waiting stood Catherine, clutching a broom.

My feet moved toward her before I could stop them.

"Princess Talia." The deep voice sliced through the moment, freezing me.

Regent Revel.

He pushed himself forward from the circle of captives. A Merchant and Artist lifted their weapons in warning. Revel barely flinched as he raised his hands in mock peace.

"How about we discuss this like civilized people," he said, his voice rough.

I straightened. "You had that chance." My voice rang across the throne room, sharp enough to draw a ripple of whispers through the crowd.

Revel's eyes narrowed.

"Where's King Madden?"

Revel's lips pressed into a tight line.

"And who," I took a deliberate step toward him, "gave you the right to rule in his place?"

Still, he said nothing.

The crowd shifted.

A man stepped forward, an older Farmer by the look of his worn brown tunic, and without hesitation, he lifted a pitchfork and pressed its tips to Revel's chest.

"Answer her," the man growled, loud enough for all to hear.

Revel's gaze remained steady. His hands stayed at his sides, even with the weapon at his chest. "The King declared war," he said flatly, voice stripped of anything but fact. "He left the city under my command. I maintained order."

Murmurs rippled through the room.

I took a step toward him. "By crowning yourself?"

"By preventing collapse," he replied, tone clipped. "I secured the city."

"Why now? Why did King Madden declare war?"

"Obsession," Revel answered without hesitation. "He saw traitors everywhere. It consumed him." His eyes shifted, cold and calculating. "He gave me orders to hold Llycia. To guard the palace. I obeyed."

"And the location of the rebel camp?" I pressed.

Revel's jaw tensed. "One of the rebels the prince had captured gave it up."

My mask slipped as confusion took hold. "Why? Who?"

"It happened after His Majesty began public executions of people he suspected were rebels. He was about to kill them when the rebel gave up the location."

My fingernails dug into my palms. "Where is that rebel now?"

"Leading the king straight to the rebel camp."

A moment passed as I processed his information.

"I've answered your questions," Revel sidestepped away from the pitchfork, but the old man countered his movement, "I'm willing for us to work this out together."

Before I could speak, Celeste's father burst forward, his voice loud and polished. "Princess Talia," he said, smiling wide, too wide. "I was against this from the beginning! I advised Revel to keep order, yes, but I never supported him crowning himself."

"You demanded the title of regent," Revel said with military coldness. "You threatened to take the support of the nobles away."

Celeste's father flushed, his hands shaking. "That's not true—I never..." He looked at me, eyes widening. "I was always against how King Madden treated you."

I didn't bother to acknowledge his lie. "You both seized power," I said, letting my words slice through the room. "And the rest of you followed."

The inner circle became still.

"Your games are finished," I said, my voice cold and clear. "Take them all to the dungeon."

The nobles and guards' protests were drowned out by the firm voices of villagers and servants as some of them, along with Adira, Eitan, and Tommy, prodded the group toward the door.

I didn't move until the last of them disappeared. A hand touched my arm, grounding me. "You handled that well," Raph murmured for only me to hear. I released a breath and barely managed a nod, still feeling the weight of it all press against my chest.

But as the doors sealed behind the prisoners, a different weight settled. Silence. Every eye in the room turned back to me. Waiting.

My throat dried up, and the throne loomed behind me.

I cleared my throat, my voice catching slightly. "I...I don't know how to thank you," I said, looking out at every face.

The older Farmer stepped forward, his pitchfork in hand. "Your Highness." He bowed. "Some of us remember when your grandparents ruled. There was...no fear, then."

A few nods followed, but the silence that followed felt awkward, unsteady. They were waiting for me to say something.

I forced my voice to stay even. "I will need some time to think," I said, lifting my chin. "Please...excuse yourselves for a moment." I extended my hand out, offering my best princess smile.

The crowd bowed their heads and shuffled out. Luckily, there was no argument.

I caught sight of Lady Astrid, Lady Marie, and Lady Olivia as they passed. They stopped briefly, offering small curtsies.

"It's really good to see you again, Your Highness," Lady Astrid said with a bright smile.

"And all of you," I replied, feeling my throat tighten. They hadn't been with the other nobles. At some point during whatever had happened here they must have left King Madden's court. "We will catch up later."

They moved on.

Catherine lingered behind them, clutching her broom like it was a sword.

Unshed tears pooled in my eyes.

She bowed. "Glad you're safe, Your Highness."

Before she straightened I wrapped my arms around her. "And me, you."

Her arms slowly wrapped around me, stiff and unsure.

"Where's Malenee?" I asked.

Her body tightened and her arms dropped.

"She...she was taken. By Prince Kasper. Many servants started disappearing."

I clutched her hands in mine. "Don't worry, we will find her. I promise."

"Thank you, Your Highness." A single tear trailed down her cheek as she dipped her head and exited the room.

Soon, it was empty, leaving Raph and me in the vast, echoing chamber.

I turned and stared at the empty throne.

Raph's voice broke the quiet. "What now?" he asked, his tone soft. "They'll expect a ruler."

I didn't look at him right away. My gaze stayed locked on the throne, and for a moment, the weight of it threatened to crush me.

"That's not me," I said, meeting his eyes. "But he'll be back," I added, my words sinking like a stone in my gut. "Madden will return."

My gaze returned to the throne. "And when he does," I said, taking a breath, "we'll be ready."

CHAPTER 28

Kasper

BLOW AFTER BLOW, REBELS collapsed at my feet, some unconscious, others dead. I didn't let my aching arms slow. I shoved forward, the fight filling my ears. Up ahead, crimson fought against rebels. If you could even call them that anymore. It was much more than a little rebellion. They fought like trained warriors, not desperate villagers. They knew the streets, and their movements were sharp and fast as they slipped between narrow alleyways.

My father's men pushed deeper, but every step forward cost us men. They weren't used to fighting on this terrain. They stumbled over loose stones and crashed against walls too tight to swing their blades freely.

I gritted my teeth. This would be a blood bath for both sides.

Smoke blurred the streets, which were thick with the scent of burning wood and iron. Shouts echoed through the streets and somewhere ahead, someone screamed for reinforcements.

I spotted a familiar figure locked in combat with two rebels—my father. A rebel lunged toward me, blade high. I didn't hesitate. I kicked him hard in the chest, sending him sprawling back into a cluster of fighters.

I ran past them, heart thudding in my ears. Every turn of the road narrowed and wound toward the mountain's base where the homes climbed higher in tight switchbacks.

I pushed my legs harder. All that mattered was getting to my father. His ship had docked first. He led the charge and was pushing toward the homes. I vaulted over a broken cart, dodged a fallen soldier, and pressed up the slope. This city was a maze of stone staircases and sharp corners, each turn another ambush waiting to spring.

My father was just ahead with only a couple of his men fighting alongside him.

A rebel blocked my path.

He was barely more than a boy, his face pale beneath the dirt and sweat. He raised his sword, hands shaking, but his eyes were fierce. He lunged. I deflected easily.

I shoved forward, using a nearby building to trap him against the wall. He stumbled back and tried to retreat.

I struck again.

He barely managed to block as his footing slipped. Panic flashed in his eyes. For a moment I saw the servant boy who my father had struck down without a thought. My sword froze. The boy in front of me wasn't a soldier. He was a terrified kid caught in a war.

My hesitation cost me, his blade slashed across my arm. It was shallow but sharp enough to burn. I hissed though my teeth, stumbling back as blood trickled down my arm.

Rage flared. More at myself than him. With a shove, I knocked his blade aside. The boy stumbled. And I drove my pommel into his temple.

He crumpled to the ground, unconscious.

I wiped the sweat from my face, ignoring the sting on my arm and forced myself up the mountain.

My father stood on a narrow path, bloodied sword in hand as a fresh wave of rebels descended from above. He was alone.

I reached him as he drove his sword through a rebel's gut. The man dropped.

"Took you long enough," my father muttered, eyes locked on the approaching rebels.

"We've lost too many. We need to fall back before we lose everything."

A sharp, humorless laugh ripped from his throat. "We'll leave when nothing but ashes remain." He raised his sword, face alight with a near manic grin.

It wasn't about power anymore. This was something else. He didn't care how many of his men died. Rage consumed him. He was lost to it. And I was drenched in blood that wasn't mine, still following him. Jules's words came back like a fresh cut. Standing next to him, I couldn't tell which one of us was worse.

The group of rebels closed in, led by an older man with sharp eyes and a steady step. He saw us, and instead of charging he raised his hand, signaling his men to bypass us.

His focus stayed on my father.

"Madden," the older rebel said, dipping his chin in a mock greeting.

My father's lips curled into a cold smile. "Still alive, old friend?" His words were laced with malice.

My mouth dropped open. It was obvious there was history between these two, but how?

"I should've known you'd be behind this," my father continued, moving toward him. "Always playing hero. Always getting in my way."

"And you," the rebel replied, voice heavy with regret, "never could let the past die."

They drew closer, eyes locked as if no one else existed.

"It's disappointing seeing you alive," my father sneered. "Though I'll enjoy ending you myself."

"It's not too late, Madden," the older rebel said in almost a whisper.

Whatever wall was between them shattered as my father gave a guttural cry. They struck at almost the same moment, and their blades collided with bone-rattling force.

I was unable to look away as they fought.

They were equals.

Their footwork and strikes were mirror images of one another. Like they'd been fighting alongside each other their whole lives. They moved up the mountain away from the main fray. I peered over my shoulder where a clash of red was matched pretty evenly with the rebels. Tightening my grasp on my sword, I followed my father and the rebel up the mountain while keeping my distance.

They reached a landing in front of a house perched on the cliffside. A woman's voice rang out, shrill with fear. "Theo! Get inside!"

A child's face flashed in the opening before the door slammed shut.

The older rebel paused briefly, blocking one of my father's strikes to look in the direction of the little boy. And his concern gave him the disadvantage. My father pushed his weight against their swords.

Dust exploded around them as the rebel staggered back. He didn't have time to regain his composure before my father attacked with an overhead strike. It was blocked, but the rebel lost his momentum. The next strike was low and a deep groan from the older rebel confirmed my suspicions. Blood had been drawn.

I moved closer. My father's back faced me, blocking the older rebel from my view, but it was obvious he was slowing from the cut he received.

My heart pounded against my ribs as the tempest inside me tore me apart. He was my biological father, yet he had never been a real father to me. Never once had he shown any love toward me. Instead, he'd killed everything or anyone I ever cared about. No matter how hard I tried to find some redeeming quality in him, there wasn't one. I used to believe he had loved my mother and blamed me for her death. It gave me hope that if he had loved once, maybe he could love again. But love wasn't something he was capable of. I wasn't even sure if it was something he had ever experienced.

The sound of skidding rocks pulled me back to the fight.

The older rebel was on one knee, breath ragged. My father stood over him, sword poised at his throat.

I knew what was coming.

CHAPTER 29

Jules

THE CITY BURNED.

Flames crawled along the wooden shop fronts, their rooftops tangled in smoke.

Every breath scraped against my throat. Bodies surged around me. Boots pounded against the ground, swords clashed, and voices rose in guttural cries. I clutched my bow tighter, forcing myself forward.

I needed to join Gil. But I couldn't stop thinking about how another village was going up in flames. Homes reduced to ashes and lives changed forever. This wasn't the change I envisioned. Not innocent blood being spilled. I couldn't help but wonder if life was better the way it was; with Madden and the callings.

I jumped back as a guard's body fell in front of me, blood spraying my boots. My stomach lurched, but I forced it down and loosed an arrow, slipping it through the gap in a guard's armor.

Gil was a couple of buildings away, releasing arrows with impossible speed. I pressed along the edge of the street, closer to the fire than the fight. The heat licked against my skin, but it kept me out of the thick of the blades.

Gil darted ahead. I caught up as he loosed another arrow, dropping a guard mid-lunge. He spun around and met my eyes, and relief covered his face. His mouth opened, but his expression darkened as he stared past me.

"What?" I asked, breathless.

He didn't answer. He stepped past me, gaze fixed somewhere beyond the smoke. I squinted up the mountain.

Two figures were locked in combat near the homes on the mountainside. The smoke thinned, and I caught a glimpse of a blade flashing in the sun. Neither man wore crimson. Gil's posture stiffened and he took another step.

"Where are you going?" I grabbed his arm.

"It's Alon," he said, barely audible. His eyes didn't leave the two figures. "He's fighting..." He trailed off.

My blood went cold. I didn't need him to name him. I knew who that sword belonged to. King Madden.

"Shouldn't we stay and fight?" I said, glancing behind us.

Gil didn't respond. His legs were already moving, his arm pulling away from me. I released a sharp breath and chased after him. The street narrowed, and smoke funneled between the mountainside houses.

Gil slowed. His hand lifted instinctively, signaling me to stop.

I crouched behind him, bow in hand, heart slamming against my ribs.

Beyond a small stone fence, King Madden and Alon circled each other. Alon's shoulders heaved. A shadow moved off to the right from the corner of a house, closer to where they fought—Kasper, his sword at his side.

My breath caught, yet it didn't seem like he had seen us.

Gil tensed beside me. He was going to move.

I grabbed his arm. He shot a glare over his shoulder, but I shook my head and pointed to the loose stones beneath our feet. One wrong step and Kasper would hear us.

Gil exhaled, then nodded once. He crept along the outer edge of the stone fence, on the grass. We carefully made our way to the edge of a house, keeping in the shadow of the overhangs.

The air was hot, but a mountain wind pulled at our clothing. We were ten paces out from where Kasper watched. Gil reached the far corner of the house and pressed his back against the wall. I followed and leaned close.

Somewhere, a woman screamed, "Theo," and then a door slammed.

My eyes flicked back to the duel. Alon staggered. Madden pressed in, merciless. Blood was drawn.

Gil withdrew an arrow, his jaw tight and eyes locked on Alon.

Alon dropped to one knee.

Gil lurched forward. I reached for the back of his tunic but grabbed air.

King Madden raised his sword. Gil surged ahead.

"No!" The word tore out of me before I could stop it.

Madden's blade lifted, poised to strike. Alon didn't look up. His eyes were closed like he'd accepted his fate. I couldn't move. Couldn't breathe. Flashes of John's dead body invaded my mind.

Madden roared.

Steel met steel.

CHAPTER 30

Kasper

MY BLADE SLAMMED INTO my father's, stopping his strike inches from the rebel's face. The jolt rattled my bones, and pain ricocheted up my arm. I'd barely made it in time. My stance was too wide, my arm too far extended, and I strained to keep the blade from slipping.

My father's eyes locked on mine, full of fury. They promised I'd regret this moment for the rest of my life.

"How dare you!" he shouted, tearing his blade free from our locked position. "Move aside!"

I stepped in front of the rebel as my father lifted his sword again, angling it to strike. "No," I said, the word low but resolute. It was the first time I'd ever told him no. My arms shook when I raised my sword again, ready for whatever came next.

"You've been a disappointment since the day you were born," he spat, his words striking harder than his blade could.

"And you've never been a father," I shot back, my breath tight and my chest heaving.

His blade came down with a roar, slicing through the air toward my head.

I blocked it in time. Metal screamed against metal.

"You're not worth the trouble anymore," he hissed, pressing me back. "Finding a new heir will be easier than suffering your failures."

The pain, shame, betrayal, and loneliness I'd buried for years rose like a tidal wave. I roared, not with fear but fury, and drove forward. "You destroyed everything I've ever loved," I said with another advance. I didn't think. I only swung. The air filled with the clash of steel and breathless rage.

My father successfully blocked every strike I threw at him, anticipating what I would do next. But he was losing his ground. He wasn't as strong as me anymore. I was slowly pushing him back, away from the rebel.

"This is for killing Duke!" I screamed, slashing my sword downward with everything I had. "And Harry!" I followed with an overhead strike. My voice cracked, the pain too much to bear, but I had to continue. Not for only myself but for everyone that had been killed by my father's hand. "For taking Lliana away from me." I swung upward and suddenly, there was no resistance.

His sword clattered to the ground, close to my feet. He was disarmed.

I pressed until the tip of my sword met the hollow of his throat. He staggered back, pinned against the wall of a house.

I had won.

And yet...I didn't feel victorious. I didn't feel anything.

I stared at him, waiting. For what, I didn't know. Maybe for him to beg. To finally see reason and promise he would change. To show a shred of remorse.

But he just looked at me, stone-cold and unmoving.

"You've taken everything from me!" My voice broke again. My hands trembled. "Did you ever love her?" The question slipped out raw and fragile.

"If you're going to kill me," he said flatly, "do it." He pushed off the wall. A drop of blood dripped down his neck where my blade pressed against his skin.

My arm shook, but I forced it to stay lifted.

He lifted a finger and pushed my sword aside like it was nothing. "She was a means to an end," he said. "The only unfortunate part of her death was leaving me with only you as an heir."

Everything inside me fractured. The truth I'd always known but never dared to believe. He had never loved anyone but himself.

He tried to step around me.

I drove my sword forward, between the gap in his armor at his ribs.

A sharp inhale escaped his lips as I released my blade. Blood coated it. I stumbled backward, and he fell to his knees, one hand clutching the wound, the other reaching uselessly for the sword he no longer had.

I stared at my sword in shock.

It was always going to end one of two ways, with my death or his, and I always figured it would be me.

"You..." he rasped, voice wet and broken. "Are going...to make...an awful king."

My heart thundered. My lungs begged for release, but I couldn't breathe.

He collapsed.

Not a king anymore. Not a father. Just...a body.

He was gone.

For a long moment, I didn't move. The sword hung limp in my hand, its tip touching the dirt. The world seemed to tilt, sound fading to a dull ring. I waited for something—relief, grief, anything—but nothing came.

I had spent my life trying to earn his approval and then trying to survive without it. Every order obeyed, every scream ignored, every line crossed in his name. And now there was nothing left to fight against. He was gone. But the question that remained terrified me. Who was I without him?

I stepped back, the fog of rage thinning. Sound returned. The world rushed back in.

I looked over my shoulder.

Jules and the blond rebel were frozen, their faces pale.

I'd expected them to escape. I hadn't expected them to witness this.

Jules's eyes flicked from the body to me. The rebel's hand moved to the hilt of his sword, but his eyes were focused down the road. The older rebel on the ground seemed to be losing consciousness.

Pulling my shoulders back, I walked toward them. The rebel stepped in front of Jules, raising his sword defensively. I didn't stop. I didn't speak. I didn't even glance in their direction. I was done fighting.

I picked up speed until I was jogging. The mountain opened below me, and I could see it all. Crimson uniforms tangled in the streets with rebels. The King's Guard were dwindling in number and had been pushed back toward the docks.

I reached the base of the mountain, drew in a breath, and screamed:

"Retreat!"

CHAPTER 31

Talia

THE ROOM SMELLED OF dust and disuse. White sheets were draped over the scattered furniture like ghosts clinging to the past. I crossed to the windows and shoved them open, letting in a breeze sharp with smoke and sea salt.

Raph pulled a sheet off a small circular table in the center of the room. We weren't meeting in the throne room. And not the ballroom, either. I'd made that clear. Not any place that reeked of King Madden.

"You sure about this room?" Raph asked, brushing dust from his hands.

"Yes." My voice hitched, making it sound like a question. "There's no trace of him here." My fingers found the pendant at my neck as I scanned the room, wondering if somewhere more official would have been better.

Raph moved toward me, gently taking my hand and lowering it from my pendant, wrapping it in his own. "It's perfect," he said quietly. "And so is your plan. Remember, you're not alone in this."

His words calmed my frantic thoughts. For the first time, it didn't feel like there were any walls between us. We were on the same side.

I gave a small nod, holding his gaze.

Footsteps echoed in the hall, and Raph gave my hand a small squeeze before stepping away. Adira and Eitan entered first, their expressions unreadable. Behind them walked an older man, Commander Brann, one of the king's former advisers. The others believed it would be good to have someone who knew how King Madden thought on the inside, but I didn't trust him. Nadav and Hafsa slipped in quietly, close behind the older man. Tommy sauntered in with a lopsided grin on his face, and Catherine trailed him, her gaze flicking across the room before landing on me.

They gathered around the table Raph stood beside, their attention shifting toward me. Silence stretched long enough I heard the birds outside.

"We'll make this quick," I said, glancing around the table. "Let's start with the palace."

Commander Brann shifted, but it was Adira who spoke first. "The nobles who claimed they no longer serve the king have been escorted off palace grounds.

Their estates are under watch." Her gaze shifted to Tommy.

"If one of them sneezes wron', y'all know abou' it," he said, smirking.

"They weren't locked up?" Commander Brann's voice cut through the room, clipped. His gaze stayed fixed on Tommy.

Nadav and Hafsa stepped in unison, closing in on him. Their presence wasn't subtle.

I held Brann's stare. "Most of them followed King Madden out of fear. They were never loyal to him. We only detained the King's Guard and those a part of the king's inner circle, as you are aware," I added, letting the weight of that settle.

His lips thinned into a tight line, but he nodded once. He knew he was walking a fine line of freedom.

"Thank you," I said to Tommy. "To all the Shades. You've done so much. If it's too much—"

"Eh, it's nothin'." He waved his hand in the air. "They're barterin' for a chance to take a watch." A laugh escaped his lips, and a small smile formed on mine.

"I should mention, uh, Your Highness..." Tommy scratched the back of his neck. "Word's spreadin'. People know you've taken hol' of the palace. Thinkin' you've claimed the throne."

All eyes turned to me. I didn't flinch, but my throat tightened.

Raph spoke up. "Now isn't the time for announcements." He glanced around the table. "Madden will return. We need to stay focused on the plan." He tilted his head in my direction.

I clasped my hands tightly behind my back. "When he comes back, I don't want him to suspect a thing. I want to catch him with his guard down."

"The kin—his guard is never down," Commander Bran said. "He'll suspect something the moment he arrives. It doesn't matter how you stage it. His paranoia has taken over. He'll be looking for betrayal."

The room tensed.

Brann shifted as he looked toward the corner of the room. "He stopped trusting his advisors. He had guards watching guards. Anyone who questioned him disappeared. He doesn't see reality, only what confirms his fears. So, if you want him to believe nothing's changed, everyone from the city to the palace will need to act like nothing has. No one breathes differently. No one dares look relieved."

Raph drew in a slow breath beside me. "Then we don't just prepare the palace, we prepare the people." He looked at Tommy who gave him a nod.

"Or you won't survive long enough to carry out whatever plan you've got brewing," Brann said.

Eitan leaned forward. "We've got scouts in the harbor and lookouts stationed at every entrance to the city. We'll know the moment he gets close."

I nodded.

"The servants and guards know their roles," Catherine said timidly. Eitan placed his hand on her shoulder and gave her an encouraging smile. Her cheeks colored slightly, but she stood taller. "They're ready," she continued. "Runners will pass messages through the halls when it begins."

Raph looked at Adira. "And our message to Aydencia?"

"It's been sent," she confirmed.

I let the quiet settle for a moment as I tried to run through everything in my head. "Anything else?" I asked.

"During the search of the palace," Adira spoke up, "we found a room that had been locked from the outside. Inside was a young woman who was barely conscious."

"Who is she?" I asked.

"Said her name was Lliana," Adira answered.

My chest tightened. "Where is she?"

"She's in the infirmary being taken care of."

I nodded, already forming a plan to go see her after this.

Eitan cleared his throat. "One more thing. I was notified before this meeting," he glanced around the table, "those who had gone missing because of Kasper have been found."

Catherine covered her mouth. "All of them?" Her eyes filled with unshed tears.

Eitan looked at her. "Yes," he said with a warm smile. "All of them."

Relief filled her face as tears spilled freely. She wrapped her arms around Eitan's waist. He remained frozen, then let out a soft breath and held her gently. A smile tugged at the corner of my mouth. I hadn't missed the way he'd jumped at the opportunity to lead that search team.

"That is wonderful news," I said, feeling my own eyes well up.

Catherine pulled away from Eitan and wiped her tears. "Where were they?"

"Beneath the palace," Eitan answered. "There's a water channel system that runs below the foundations. They were kept in a small chamber."

"Make sure they're cared for," I said.

Eitan nodded. "Already arranged."

"Good," I said, straightening my shoulders. "Everyone is dismissed, for now."

Their feet shuffled as they began to leave. Hafsa and Nadav followed Commander Brann out the door. Adira and Tommy exchanged some words on their way out. Eitan hovered near Catherine, so close she brushed his arm when passing. He looked like he might follow her out, but she hesitated by the door.

"Your Highness," she said gently. "There's something you need to know." Her hands were clasped so tightly I saw her knuckles strain beneath her skin.

My stomach turned.

Raph came to stand next to me.

Catherine fidgeted with the hem of her sleeve. "Before King Madden declared war on the rebel camp, he brought a handful of prisoners into the throne room. People he accused of having loyalties to the rebels."

My breath caught.

"He started killing them one by one. Just—" She broke off, covering her mouth. "There were no trials, no proof. He wanted to send a message." She dropped her head. "I was next in line."

I stepped toward her.

"He was going to kill me," she whispered, tears brimming in her eyes. "But your father...." Her voice broke, seeming to be unable to finish.

My lungs felt tight. I didn't want to hear this. Raph's hand found mine.

"My father?" I whispered.

Tears ran silently down her cheeks. Terror slid down my spine like ice. She finally met my eyes. "It happened so fast." Her voice cracked. "Madden. He...he killed him."

I stilled. Catherine's lips continued moving, but I couldn't hear her. The room fell away. The floor. The walls. My vision tunneled.

Raph's arm encircled me, but I barely felt it.

Gone.

Air wouldn't move into my lungs. Nothing seemed to move.

My father was gone.

A sob clawed its way up my throat, and I shook my head as if denial could rewrite the truth.

"No," I whispered, but the word broke apart.

Raph pulled me close, and I collapsed into him, my hands gripping the fabric of his shirt like it was the only thing tethering me to this world. My knees hit the floor and Raph went with me, holding me as my body shook with sobs I couldn't contain.

It couldn't be true. Madden wouldn't have harmed him. Use him as bait, yes, but...

Mother. How was I supposed to tell her? It felt like I had been split in half.

Catherine knelt nearby, crying quietly. "I'm so sorry," she said.

I sobbed.

Time blurred. By the time I could catch my breath the light from the windows had dimmed.

The pain was sharp and deep, but beneath it something else stirred. A flicker. A spark.

I pushed back from Raph, my hands shaking. His eyes were filled with sorrow.

"My father didn't die for nothing," I said, my voice low and hoarse. My heart felt cracked wide open, like it would never be whole again. But I'd make sure my father's death brought the change he and Mother had always dreamed of for Landore.

"Madden may have started this war," I continued, "but we'll decide how it ends." A fresh breeze tore through the room. "And I'll be ready for him."

CHAPTER 32

Jules

THE ACADEMY DOORS SWUNG shut behind us with a heavy thud, and I finally exhaled. I looked down at my hands. Blood was dried under my nails and crusted in the creases of my palms. Some of it was Alon's. Some...I didn't know.

Outside, the wind carried the scent of ash and sea, but it was quiet, eerily so compared to the chaos we had left behind. The quiet made it worse somehow, like the city was holding its breath. Inside, the halls were full of injured warriors, groans, and shouting. Alon had been one of the first we brought in, bleeding and barely conscious. The physician's grave expression still clung to me.

Gil led us away from the academy, which looked more like a palace. The door we had exited led to what seemed to be some sort of training grounds as the morning sun highlighted the different equipment and an area with targets set up. Gil didn't stop until he came to a raised platform. He leaned against one of the wooden poles supporting it and dragged his red-stained hand down his face.

We'd spent the night hauling in injured, searching for space for them where there was none. I could still hear the cries and screams as if I were right there again. Talia's mother was in the midst of it all, scurrying from cot to cot. I'd wanted to go to her, to throw my arms around her, to tell her everything. But how could I? How could I look her in the eye and say her husband was gone?

"There was so much blood," Gil said, pulling me back.

"I know." My voice caught. "But it's over."

His gaze flicked to mine. "Is it?"

I hesitated. "They're gone, at least. The King's Guard. Kasper. They retreated..."

"But will they stay gone?"

I didn't have an answer.

Gil sighed and looked out toward the trees. "No plan. No Alon. And half the warriors in Aydencia are dead or injured. We survived yesterday. That's all."

I glanced toward the doors, then lowered my voice. "But King Madden is dead." Gil didn't move. We hadn't told anyone yet how King Madden died, but no one had asked. Everyone was too busy with the injured and assessing the damage. "Kasper killed him. That has to mean—"

Gil's head turned sharply toward me. "It doesn't mean anything. We have no idea what Kasper is thinking. He could have called a retreat to go back to Llycia and regroup to attack again. They know where we are," he dropped his gaze, "and it's my fault."

"Stop," I said, reaching for his arm.

He stared at the ground. "There are so many dead, Jules." His voice cracked. "Some were so young."

I placed my hand against his chest. "You didn't cause this. King Madden did. He was the one who declared war."

Gil looked at me, the jokes and bravado he hid behind were completely gone. "I led them here. I gave them the path."

"You didn't have a choice. He was going to kill them." I met his eyes, voice low. "This war was inevitable. And Aydencia was ready. They fought back."

His shoulders sagged and he looked away, blinking hard. "It doesn't feel like it was worth it."

His words echoed inside me as if I had spoken them. I would never believe war was the right answer. With all that destruction, it couldn't be. But I was done being buried beneath the ruins of King Madden's reign. "Maybe it never will," I admitted. "But you can't let this guilt stop you. It's time to move forward. To help build something out of the ashes. Something better."

He met my eyes again. I could see the guilt there, but also something else. Resolve.

I reached for his hand and intertwined our fingers. "We will make sure this doesn't happen again."

He nodded. "We need a plan."

"Once Alon is awake, we will tell him what happened. He will have a plan," I said, squeezing his hand. "Plus, didn't that captain tell you Talia left a week ago with Raph, Nadav, and Hafsa for Nefali?"

"Yeah," he said.

"They'll get Nefali's support and Kasper won't stand a chance if he tries anything."

The side of Gil's mouth lifted slightly, but it was all I needed. He looked at our joined hands. "Thank you," he said softly.

I nodded, my throat too tight to answer audibly.

We stood there in silence as the sun climbed above the tree line.

For the first time, I didn't feel like I had to be the one to fix everything. I didn't have the answers and that was okay, because I wasn't alone.

I wasn't the only one fighting.

CHAPTER 33

Talia

"MOST OF THE RESCUED are recovering well, Your Highness." Gale tightened his arm around Malenee's waist as he finished his report.

Every time I looked at her, my eyes watered, and I wasn't the only one. Catherine clung to Malenee's free hand like it was a lifeline.

The room still smelled faintly of dust, even after four days of meetings. The once-forgotten space had become our makeshift war room. Someone had removed the white sheets from the furniture, and the windows were cracked open, letting in the early spring air, but an eerie silence clung to the walls like a held breath.

"However," Gale spoke again, "some are weaker than others. Would it be possible to move them to the Healer's wing?"

"Of course," I said. "Whatever they need. I'm just glad you're all safe."

"We are too, Your Highness." A tear slipped down Malenee's cheek.

Raph stood beside me, arms crossed, his eyes flicking to the open doorway like he was waiting for something to happen.

Adira appeared. Her eyes were sharp as she walked in. "They're here."

The air seemed to vanish.

"Ships have been spotted in the harbor," she continued. "At least four. They will be docking soon."

Every eye was on me, waiting for an answer I didn't feel qualified to give. But my heart didn't pound like I expected it to. I felt a strange calm descend over me, the kind that came before a storm. I nodded to Adira. "Warn the others," I said. "It's starting."

They gave tight nods and quietly disappeared.

Raph turned to me. "You sure you're ready?"

I met his gaze. "Yes."

His jaw clenched. "I don't like it."

"I know," I said, seeing the fight in his eyes. The warrior in him screamed to shield me, but the man in him was learning to let me stand on my own.

He lowered his forehead to mine. My breath caught. We hadn't had any moments alone. There hadn't been time for us to even discuss what came next.

"If you need me—"

"I know," I said, barely above a whisper.

"I'll be right outside those doors, listening."

"And you'll wait? Like I asked."

He didn't answer. He leaned in and kissed me, soft and lingering. He pulled away too soon. "We should go."

We walked in silence to the throne room, guards stiff as we passed. It felt like the palace held its breath. Not knowing what today would bring, just that it would change everything. At the doors, Raph grabbed my hand. "Be careful. Don't let him get too close."

I offered a faint smile. "I won't."

"I could hide behind the dais. He wouldn't kno–"

I squeezed his hand. "No. It needs to be me and him."

He stared at me a moment longer. "Okay."

He opened the doors. I slipped inside. They closed with a soft thud behind me, the sound echoing through the throne room like a final note. Everything felt too still.

I climbed the dais and paused at the top. My chest tightened as I lowered myself onto the throne. It felt wrong. But I couldn't show that. I straightened and the minutes passed.

A guard finally popped his head in. "They've entered the palace and have been notified of Lieutenant Revel's request."

"Thank you."

The guard disappeared. I steadied my breathing and gave one last glance to the door where Raph waited. The air around me thickened. Every tick of silence stretched thin until—footsteps.

The double doors opened with a screech and Kasper stepped in. Alone.

Our eyes locked.

"Where is your father?" I asked. "What are you doing here?" he asked. Our voices collided, the words hanging awkwardly between us.

He moved in, closing the distance.

I rose, my pulse thrumming.

"Where is Lieutenant Revel?" he asked between long strides.

"Where is King Madden?" I fired back.

His lips pressed together.

"Revel is in the dungeon with those loyal to the king. We've taken control of the palace."

He stopped a few strides from the base of the dais. No emotion crossed his face. Heat traveled up my neck at the lack of knowing what he was thinking.

"Now, where is your father?" I demanded one more time.

A flicker of something crossed his face. It vanished before I could name it. "He didn't survive," he said as if it was common news. "Killed in battle."

I stared, not able to fully accept what he was saying. When I spoke, my voice came out louder than I intended. "King Madden is dead?" My legs buckled and I sank onto the throne, the weight of his words crashing over me. "But that would mean you're—"

The doors flung open. Raph stormed in with guards behind him, swords drawn.

Kasper whirled, drawing his blade.

"Stop!" I jumped to my feet, racing down the steps. "Wait!"

Raph and the guards had Kasper surrounded.

Kasper's eyes darted back to me. "I don't want trouble," he said. "You can have the palace. The throne. All of it."

Raph scoffed. "And we're supposed to trust you?"

I squeezed through the circle of guards surrounding Kasper and stood next to Raph. He stepped forward, but I placed my hand out and shook my head. With a tense look he stayed behind me.

"Why should we trust you?" I asked, turning to Kasper.

Kasper's gray eyes shot through me. "Because...I'm finally free." He tossed his sword to the floor. It clattered against the stone.

I stared at him, trying to read through his words. There was something different about him. His face was more open. Softer somehow. Or maybe broken. But his words spoke to my own heart. Because a sense of freedom was exactly what I felt when he said King Madden was dead.

"All I want is to make sure Lliana is safe." His eyes pleaded with me.

I'd never fully understand Lliana's and his relationship, but after talking with her, I knew they cared for each other deeply. "Lower your swords," I said.

The guards hesitated.

"Do it," I said again, looking at Raph.

He lowered his and the rest followed.

"Tell us what happened," I said.

Kasper's shoulders sagged. "Can we speak privately?"

"No," Raph said instantly.

"Yes," I said, not looking away from Kasper.

I looked at the guards. "Leave us."

They obeyed, but Raph stayed. I didn't mind, because I wanted him there. I may have believed Kasper's words, but he could still have something up his sleeve.

Kasper stepped closer to us once the doors shut. "We weren't prepared for what the rebel camp was. However, nothing was going to stop him from attacking. We made it to land, but it was clear we were outnumbered. Many lives were being lost." He rubbed the back of his neck slowly. "I found my father working his way up the mountain toward the homes. He was fighting a lone older rebel, they seemed to have some sort of history."

Raph and I shared a look but let Kasper continue. "I stayed hidden in the shadows nearby. I could see my father wasn't going to stop. Not until he killed him or died trying. He drew first blood, and the older rebel lost ground… I don't know what came over me," Kasper said, eyes far away. "I stepped in. I couldn't watch him take another life, not after—" His eyes flicked to me and then he lowered them to the floor. My throat tightened. "He had to be stopped, and I knew I was the only one that could do it."

"You killed him," I whispered.

He kept his gaze low. "Yes."

"Who else knows?" Raph asked.

"Not sure." His voice caught.

"Your men?" Raph pressed.

"No. They think he died at the hands of a rebel."

"So what do we do now?" I asked, looking between them.

Kasper's eyes met mine. "I've given it some thought. I was hoping we could come to an accord of sorts."

"An accord?" I asked, lifting my eyebrows.

"Yes." His voice didn't waver. "Me and you."

CHAPTER 34

Talia

I STOOD OUTSIDE THE massive ballroom doors, heart thudding in a quiet rhythm. I couldn't forget the other two times I'd stepped into that room, first, when Madden declared me the lost princess and then on my forced wedding day. And here I was, about to face hundreds of people waiting to hear what would come next for Landore. I tugged at the tight sleeves of the dress that was designed specifically for this day. It was elegant and uncomfortable, lavender silk, threaded with silver in swirling patterns. Hopefully, it would be the last dress like this I'd ever have to wear. The thought put a small jolt of courage in me. This time, I'd be walking in by choice.

"Ready?" I asked.

"Not even a little," Kasper replied from beside me, tugging on the collar of his shirt. He was dressed in a fitted black overcoat and dark trousers. No crown or fancy embroidery.

"Well, it can't be as bad as your speech in Gasmere."

His head snapped toward me. "You heard about that?"

I muffled a laugh. "Everyone heard about that."

Kasper muttered something under his breath. "Where's your bodyguard?" he asked half-joking.

"Whatever issues you two have," I said, eyeing him, "you need to get over them."

He shrugged with mock indifference.

"And don't worry," I added with a grin. "He's always close."

A beat passed.

"How's Lliana?" I asked softly, wondering if she would make an appearance.

His gaze dropped to the floor. "I don't know if she'll ever be the same. Or if we will…"

I reached for his arm and gave it a light squeeze. "Don't give up on her. She needs time. Both of you do."

He met my eyes, but they were dull, with dark circles underlining them. The past two months had exhausted everyone, but Kasper had carried the worst of it. Not only trying to piece the kingdom back together, but also convince everyone he wasn't his father. That he had changed.

Before he could reply, a guard approached with a bow, then awkwardly corrected himself with a slight nod. "They're ready for you."

Kasper offered his arm. I nodded, placing my hand on his. Together, we faced the doors, which opened with a slow, echoing groan.

The ballroom shimmered with morning light which poured through the domed glass ceiling, casting warm golden rays across the marble floors. The candelabras around the perimeter and balcony remained unlit but still glinted softly. A breeze circled the room through the open floor-to-ceiling windows.

Kasper led me down the center aisle, which had been kept clear for our entrance. Color bloomed everywhere with nobles in silks and villagers in their finest. Most of them stood on opposite sides of the room. Old prejudices would take time to die.

Movement caught my eye. A small child bounced on her toes—Jemma. She spotted me and tugged on Jarred's sleeve while waving wildly. I pulled away from Kasper before remembering what I was doing. I smiled and gave a small wave back as we passed. The Colans and Gradys stood clustered around them. It was good to see them again, but also strange. So much had changed since my time in Hattlee. It felt like a different life. But one I would always cherish. I hadn't known it then, but there were parts of myself, my true self, that had been fighting to break out and be seen.

With every step we took, the room pulsed with excitement. Closer to the dais, Cyrus stood beside my mother. She wore a sapphire tunic embroidered with gold thread. Her brown hair was braided and coiled at the nape of her neck. Strength radiated from her like always, but behind her eyes was a shadow I knew too well. Grief. We exchanged a small smile. We both knew Father would be proud of the direction Landore was headed in, but knowing didn't ease the ache. I wasn't sure if the pain would ever leave me, or that I wanted it to.

The leaders of Aydencia were to the left of the dais where Alon stood tall like he'd never been wounded, with Richard and Hanna. Surprisingly, it hadn't taken much convincing to get them on board with our plan. The war seemed to have shifted their perspective. Even Richard apologized to me for his actions, a handful of times. Hafsa and Nadav were beside them as poised as ever. They would be leaving for Nefali tomorrow, but would be back soon as they agreed to be liaisons between Nefali and Landore.

On the right side of the aisle were Tommy and a few of the Shades. Many of them had been open to being adopted, and were living with families in different villages. Ahead of them were Adira, Eitan, Gil, and Jules. Jules's eyes found mine, steady and sure. She didn't smile. She didn't wave. She simply lifted her chin as if to say, *you've got this.*

Kasper and I climbed the first steps of the dais, and from the corner of my eye I caught Raph shift forward from the crowd, taking position at the base of the platform. A smile tugged at the corner of my mouth. At the top, we turned and faced the room.

For a moment, I stood there and took it in. These people had made a difference, not only in my life, but in the future of Landore. They hadn't been afraid to rise up and fight for change.

Kasper released my hand and stepped forward. I took a slow breath in, feeling the weight of what would come next. The room hushed. Most of the villagers' eyes widened and some seemed to shift back. I took a small step closer to him.

"Citizens of Landore," Kasper began. "Our kingdom will never know peace unless it becomes unified again." His voice carried across the room. "And that's something neither I nor Talia can do alone."

No one in the room moved or gave any sign of support.

"Which is why today, together," he glanced back at me, "we announce the end of the monarchy."

Gasps erupted from the crowd, mainly from the nobles' side of the room. Whispers rose like a gust of wind. Kasper held steady. "Change must come. We believe Landore's future lies not in bloodlines, but in wisdom and courage. With those chosen to lead, not born to it. From this day forward, Landore will be governed by a council of representatives from across the kingdom."

The chatter grew louder.

"How can we trust your word?"

"Who are these representatives?"

Kasper's back stiffened at the barrage.

I stepped forward. "We know this is a big change. Maybe a frightening one. But the truth is, the change has already begun. You're living it. Some of you even started it. And Kasper and I believe *you* deserve to lead it and build Landore into something new." I let myself scan the room. "This change will take time. We will serve on the council temporarily, to help lay the foundation. But Landore doesn't need another king or queen. It needs its people to bring it into the future."

Applause sparked in pockets, then grew, but some still stood with skeptical faces. Kasper and I shared a look, and he raised a hand to silence the room. "Today, we welcome the first members of the new Landorian Council."

I called them forward one by one. "Marie Grady. Cyrus Thorne. Laraine Fenwick. Eitan Corven. Garron

Hale." They stepped out from the crowd and made their way to the dais.

I fought back tears, watching the people of Landore and of Aydencia become one unit. I was especially excited Garron agreed to serve on the council. He was the young man who I had caught talking with Richard. He had overseen Aydencian's civic affairs, and I knew he would fight for the people to be heard.

"These men and women have committed to serving for the next three years," I said. "To represent your voices, your hopes, for a better tomorrow. After the three years, new representatives will be chosen by the people of Landore."

Applause and a few cheers broke out.

Kasper spoke when they quieted. "Our first order of business will be to continue rebuilding villages, making them strong again. We will also continue reviewing the calling system." Hushed conversations picked up again. "We know you have questions. We don't have all the answers yet. But this is the start, and we are committed to listening and establishing something stronger than what we had before." He paused. "In the meantime, let us celebrate the future of Landore." He extended his arms as music and cheers filled the room.

Aunt Laraine gave me a quick wink as she and the other council members stepped down from the dais to greet the people. The crowd broke apart into smaller groups. Long tables piled with food and drinks lined the edges of the room. The atmosphere was no longer thick with tension, but hummed with life.

Kasper lingered beside me at the base of the dais for a moment before a cluster of nobles pulled him aside. No doubt worried about titles and what would become of them. I did not envy him explaining there'd no longer be a need for a court, but how there would be other ways they could serve Landore and its people.

"You did wonderfully," my mother said, eyes shimmering.

She opened her arms, and I walked into them, letting the tension melt from my shoulders. For a moment we didn't speak. She simply held me. I pulled back to look at her and her hands cupped my face. "Your father would be so proud."

I swallowed hard. "Thank you."

Before either of us could say more, a high voice cut through the noise. "Talia!" Jemma barreled through the crowd, her braid bounding behind her. Jarred chased after her, trying to act like he wasn't running.

"You were amazing!" Jemma cried, throwing her arms around my waist. "Like a real-life warrior queen—except for the queen part, I guess." I laughed, hugging her back.

Jarred reached us with a wide grin.

"Wow, Jarred, have you grown?" I asked. The little boy I remembered was now almost to my chest. His face lit up.

"Don't remind him," Jemma said, releasing me from her hug to cross her arms and give an eyeroll. "He never stops rubbing it in." Mother and I shared a hidden smile.

Behind Jarred, the Colans and Gradys caught up.

"Ms. Caffrey. Mrs. Caffrey," Mr. Colan said warmly.

"It's good to see you again, dear," Mrs. Colan said, wrapping me in a quick hug.

She released me, but Mrs. Grady was right behind her with arms extended.

"It's good to see all of you," I said, refusing to let the tears fall. "Have you met my mother, Laurel?"

"Yes," Mr. and Mrs. Colan said at the same time. I scrunched my eyebrows.

"I sought them out the moment they entered the palace," my mother said. "With everything that happened to Hattlee, I thought they might be in need of extra hands." She smiled sheepishly at me.

"That's a brilliant idea," I said, ignoring the tug on my heart from her not telling me.

"We're honored to have you," Mrs. Colan gave her a smile.

"And I've been giving that clinic idea of yours some thought. I think it could be great for the village," Mr. Colan added.

"Clinic?" I asked, looking from the Colans to my mother.

Mother answered first. "I thought a clinic may generate some interest for new Healers for Hattlee."

I was stunned. "That would be exactly what Hattlee needs." My mother's face lit up.

They continued in conversation about how the potential clinic could work, but I stood there only half listening. A part of me was excited for this opportunity for my mother, but a part of me also thought she would be staying in Llycia with me for a while. However, I knew she needed this. She needed a way to give back. To find her purpose again.

Kasper caught my eye across the room. He was surrounded by a group of nobles. He gave me a strained look, before answering one of them. I stifled a laugh. I had a feeling he would be taking his leave from this party fairly soon.

"Yes, we are excited for this next chapter in Llycia," Mrs. Grady said, answering mother's question. "Even though we will miss the Colans terribly." Mrs. Colan and Mrs. Grady shared a side hug.

Jemma jumped into the conversation. "Mrs. Grady said I could come and stay with them for a bit."

"Yes, after they get settled," Mrs. Colan said, emphasizing the last part.

Mrs. Grady turned to me. "I truly can't tell you how honored I am. We are all," she glanced at Mr. Grady and Jarred, "excited to serve the people of Landore."

"Yes, thank you," Mr. Grady added.

I opened my mouth, but Mr. Colan cut in.

"I can't believe you're going to let this guy into Llycia," he joked, nudging Mr. Grady with his shoulder.

Mr. Grady punched him back. "Just admit you're going to miss me."

"Never," Mr. Colan said with a suppressed smile.

Laughter broke out within the group.

"We're grateful you accepted," I said as the laughter died down.

"Mother, there's cake," Jemma exclaimed, pointing to one of the far tables. "We have to get some before it's all gone." She tugged on her parents' arms.

"Sorry," they said with a smile. Both families made their way toward the food.

Mother shifted as I felt another presence come beside me.

Raph appeared with his hand extended. "Excuse me, Princess," he said with mock-seriousness. "May I have this dance?"

I was about to object since no one was dancing. But the music swelled, and couples paired off in front of us. I peered at my mother, who gave me a knowing smile.

"I think I better go check on Cyrus," she said, taking her leave.

Raph stood in front of me with his hand extended. I lifted my hand and froze midair. "Only if you stop calling me *Princess*," I said.

He grabbed my hand and pulled me in close, leading me in the dance before I could object. "Whatever you say, Caffrey," he whispered in my ear.

My breath caught as he spun me in a circle.

We joined the other couples on the dance floor, and I relaxed into Raph's arms, letting him lead me. I observed the people, taking in their expressions of merriment. All of the planning over the past two months seemed to have paid off. I could feel the weight lift from my shoulders. My role as "princess" wasn't over yet, but I could almost taste the freedom that would come soon.

By the tables, Eitan tried to convince Catherine to taste something. She shook her head, then smiled and did it anyway. They'd both be staying at the palace. Eitan's one request for accepting his position as a representative was that he could still volunteer his free time in the kitchen. Catherine stepped up to take on the role as head housekeeper.

Adira stood further back from them against the wall, finding solitude in the shadows. A nobleman angled toward her, but she quickly disappeared among the sea of people before he had the chance to approach. She'd spent the past two months helping with the adoption of some of the Shades and would be taking a handful of them back with her to Aydencia, Tommy included. They'd attend Aydencia Academy, Landore's first official academy. Open to all to go and receive an education. Adira had taken Raph's old role as the combat teacher.

A burst of laughter pulled my eye to Jules's parents with Gil. Mr. Varnier clapped him on the back like an old friend. Jules stood behind them, arms folded, trying not to smile, and failing miserably. She looked my way, and I gave her one of Gil's signature winks. Her cheeks darkened as she narrowed her eyes, but then Gil swept her into his arms and led her to the dance floor. She broke out in laughter. Warmth spread through my chest. She might be trying to deny her feelings for Gil, but she was breaking. They'd been away for most of the time, traveling from village to village helping rebuild. There was much work to be done, and they'd volunteered to be at the forefront of it all.

The music softened into a slower tune, but Raph's hand remained strong against the small of my back, his other still curled around mine. He cleared his throat. I looked up, not realizing how close our faces had gotten.

His eyes flicked to my lips and back to my eyes. He leaned away. "So," he said slowly. "I've been thinking..."

Something about the way he spoke sent a ripple through me. "Okay?"

"I would like to ask you something." He swallowed.

Everything inside of me tightened. "Yes…"

His mouth opened. Then closed. Something fluttered in my chest, fragile and breathless. We had stopped dancing, but he still held me.

He stepped back, just enough to look at me fully. "I was wondering if you would—obviously when you're done with the council and everything—" he gushed. "I was wondering if you would come with me?"

I blinked. "Come with you?"

"Traveling," he said quickly, stumbling a bit over his words. "With the borders open again, I plan to see the other kingdoms. To explore the places we've only heard stories about, and who knows, maybe discover if there is anything beyond the four kingdoms."

I stared at him.

He shifted again. "I mean…only if you want to. I figured…maybe, when all this is over…"

I exhaled. "Yes."

His brows lifted.

"Yes," I repeated. "I would love to go anywhere with you."

The tension in his shoulders melted. A smile curved across his face, lopsided and relieved. He pulled me closer, and we rejoined the dance. Everything seemed to blur in the background as glee overtook me.

For the first time, I wasn't worried or fearful about my future. I was excited. I had no idea what could happen over the next few years, but I was ready to figure it out.

To discover my future.

IF YOU ENJOYED THE RISING PLEASE HELP MY AUTHOR JOURNEY BY LEAVING A REVIEW!

Amazon

Goodreads

StoryGraph

ACKNOWLEDGMENTS

It's hard to believe I'm writing the final acknowledgements page for The Calling series. What a journey it's been. When I first started writing *The Calling*, I never imagined how deeply readers would connect with these characters, or how far this story would take me. Finishing The Calling series has been one of the most humbling, emotional, and rewarding experiences of my life. I'm filled with so much excitement at seeing where this series will go now that it is finished.

To my readers: Your love for this series has kept me going more times than you know. Your emails, messages, reviews, and excitement over plot twists reminded me how important this story was. Your belief in these characters helped me believe in them too, even when I hit creative roadblocks. Thank you for sticking with me and the characters through every trial and triumph. You made it possible to reach the end. I truly couldn't have done this without you.

All glory is due to God. He continues to give me the words, the heart, and the calling to write. I'm constantly in awe of the stories He allows me to tell.

To my husband and our two boys: your support has meant everything to me. Thank you for cheering me on every step of the way, even when I wanted to throw in the towel.

To my Street Team: I don't have the words to express how grateful I am. You've walked beside me through each book, offering not just support but friendship. Thank you for being patient when life slowed the process and thank you for loving this series with such contagious passion.

To my beta reader and developmental editor, Jade Lawson: your insight has been invaluable since the beginning of this series. I'm endlessly thankful for you and your willingness to help me shape and evolve this story. It wouldn't be what it is without you.

To my editor, Brittany Ortega at E&A Editing Services: I'm so glad we got to close out the series together. Your keen eye, encouragement, and faith in my writing have helped shape this final book into something I'm proud of. Thank you for always believing in me and this story.

And finally, to anyone who has supported The Calling series: thank you. Thank you for letting this story into your heart. I hope you carry a piece of it with you, wherever your story leads next.

With so much love and gratitude,

L.C. Pye

About Author
L.C. Pye

L.C. Pye is a Montana-based author of YA novels. She grew up in North Dakota, then moved to Australia for four years after college. She met her husband there, and in 2018, they moved to the Carolinas where they started their family. Now she resides in Montana with her husband and three beautiful kids.

She has spent most of her life creating stories through the art of dance. But after a dream in 2019, she decided to try telling her stories through words.

L.C. has had the privilege of traveling to many different countries, and she loves to put those differing but beautiful cultures into her writing. She hopes all her readers will experience the same beauty she has.

Connect with L.C.

Website: www.lcpye.com
Instagram: @l.c.pye
TikTok: @l.c.pye
Email: authorl.c.pye@gmail.com

9 798987 974674